Jade's Dilemma
Lead Us Not Into Temptation

a novel by Reign

Dreams Books
Dreams Publishing Company
www.dreamspublishishing.com

Dreams Publishing Company
Post Office Box 4731
Rocky Mount, North Carolina 27803
www.DreamsPublishing.com

© 2006 by Reign

Dreams Titles are available at special quantity discounts for bulk purchases for sales promotion, premiums, fund-raising, educational, or institutional use. Special book excerpts or customized printings can also be created to fit specific needs. For details, write to:
Dreams Publishing Company, Post Office Box 4731, Rocky Mount, North Carolina 27803; Attention: Special Sales.

Cover Designed by Nicki Angela
Cover illustration by Larry Russell
ISBN 0-9770936-5-4

Library of Congress Control Number (LCCN): 2006924656

1. Family & Relationships – Love & Romance
2. African American Women – Fiction
3. Interpersonal Relationships

First Dreams Books Printing: October 2006

10 9 8 7 6 5 4 3 2 1

Manufactured in the United States of America

Dedication

This book is dedicated to Ava, born July 19, 2005.

Acknowledgements

As always, I wish to first thank my Father and my God through Christ Jesus who is my light and my salvation.

To my cousin, Sula Kirksey, you are more than family, you are my friend.

To Julie Joyner, thanks for giving me the facts.

To my proofreaders, Betty Joyner, Hope Phillips and Teresa Rhodes, thank you for all that you do.

To my editor, Jeannette Cezanne, (Dr. J.), we work so well together.

To my PR, Robin Caldwell, thanks for wanting me to look good!

To my sister in Christ, Cassandra Williams, thanks for promoting the Dilemma Series in your hair salon.

To my husband Calvin, I thank God for allowing you to find me.

Matthew 18:21 Then came Peter to him, and said, Lord, how oft shall my brother sin against me, and I forgive him? till seven times?

Matthew 18:22 Jesus saith unto him, I say not unto thee, Until seven times: but, Until seventy times seven.

PROLOGUE

Jade opened her front door and her heart sank. "Oh, my God, not again!"

Her home had been ransacked. Jade's friend Sheena pushed in front of her to get a good look at the disarray, while at the same time reaching for the cell phone in her purse.

Jade didn't know where to look. Destruction was everywhere. She wandered into her bedroom, seeing that the contents of the drawers had been emptied onto the floor. "This makes the second time in three months, Sheena," she said with a sigh. "I don't *have* anything. Why do they keep messing with me?" She spoke so softly that Sheena could barely hear her.

The two women had known each other since they were teenagers. It was easy for Sheena to identify the mixture of frustration and sadness that clouded her friend's golden brown face. Just moments before, Jade had been overjoyed as she told Sheena about the ninety-seven she had just received on the examination she had taken in her Judicial Politics class.

Now Sheena's voice was terse as she spoke into her cell phone. "Yes, I want to report a burglary at 2431 Wainwright Street. It's in the Fairview Manor section of Camden." Sheena walked to the door of Jade's bedroom. "Don't touch anything," Sheena cautioned her. "Maybe they can get some fingerprints this time."

"Prints? These people are professionals. You can be sure they used gloves." Jade moved past Sheena and walked toward her son's bedroom. "Oh, no!" Desmond's television was gone.

Again.

She blew out a long sigh. "I need to call Darrell and tell him not to bring Desmond home."

"Too late," she heard a familiar voice say. Jade spun around, literally bumping into Darrell, who had entered the house unnoticed behind them.

"The police are on the way," Sheena informed them, snapping her phone shut and reaching to take Desmond from Darrell's arms. "Hey, there, Dee! Come on, let Aunty Sheena take you into the living room."

Jade tried – and failed – to stop the tears from rolling down her cheeks. Darrell opened his arms to her and she couldn't resist walking into the warmth of his embrace. Then the floodgates opened and she began sobbing openly. "I'm so sorry. I don't mean to be a baby."

"No, I'm sorry," Darrell said, stroking her back. "I shouldn't have let you stay here after the first time this happened."

"It's not your fault." Her face was still buried in his chest. *How could I allow myself to lose control like this?* Jade wondered. She had always been a strong woman. In the past, a blow like this would have been nothing to take. *I've been through worse! What's wrong with me?*

Darrell's voice rumbled against her ear. "Yes it is. My job is to protect you and my son, and I'm not doing a very good job of it at all."

Jade leaned back and looked up at him. "But it's *not* your job. I'm not your responsibility."

"Yes it is, and yes you are," he said gently. "And you're *not* staying here another night."

She stepped out of his embrace. "You're right. I don't need to stay here. I'm going to call my mother. I'm sure she'll let us stay with her." Jade turned and joined Sheena and Desmond in the living room. "Can I use your cell phone?"

"Sure," Sheena answered, reaching into her purse.

Darrell had followed Jade into the room and now he shook his head. "I really don't think that's a good idea."

Jade hesitated before pressing in her mother's number. "Why?"

"Well, for one, how are you going to commute from Sicklerville to Camden?"

Jade thought for a moment. It was almost a half hour drive from her mother's house in Sicklerville to the Rutgers University's Camden Campus. "That's not a problem. I have a car, and I can also get the train. The Broadway terminal is only a few blocks away from campus."

He looked impatient. "Yeah, but it's not practical."

"Well, you know you can stay with me," Sheena offered.

Darrell looked at Sheena. "No, she's going to stay in my house."

Jade gasped. "Are you crazy? I can't stay with you!"

"I didn't say you were going to stay with me. I'm going to move in with my parents. You and Dee can live in my house."

Jade was feeling stubborn. "I can't do that."

"Yes, you can. My house is just around the corner from my parents and since Mom takes care of Dee while you're in school, it's more convenient for you and for me. Besides, Dee's room is already set up there. It's already his home."

"Well, it may be home for Dee, but not for me."

"Jade, don't make this difficult. I didn't just think of this. I should have done this the first time you were robbed. But you insisted on doing everything on your own."

Jade leaned her back against the wall. "That's because I don't want to have to depend on anyone."

"Well, we did this your way, now it's time to try it my way." He sounded reasonable.

Jade knew Darrell was right about the commute. With gas prices rising, it was sure to be a burden. She looked over at Sheena, still holding Desmond. "I don't know, Darrell, people are going to talk."

"So, let them! Besides, they're already talking." Darrell took her hand. "Look, we've done nothing wrong. It doesn't matter to me what people think. I only care what God thinks."

Sheena cleared her throat. "I think he's right, Jade. It would take you five minutes to drop off Dee in the mornings. That means you'll have a little more time for yourself."

Darrell smiled. "So, it's settled. You and Dee move into my house and I'll move in with my parents. This way, I don't have to worry about you anymore."

There was a loud knock at the door and a call of "police!"

"Well, that was quick!" Sheena went to answer the door.

Darrell turned to Jade. "Come on; let's give the report so we can get out of here."

CHAPTER ONE
More than a year later...

The first week of the spring semester had been tiring for Jade. And it wasn't even over. She had to get started on a question that was due Monday morning.

"Don't let him stay up too late!" she yelled out to Darrell from the door.

"I promised you I wouldn't this time, didn't I?" Darrell yelled back. "Say 'bye to Mommy, Dee." Desmond vigorously waved his little hand goodbye and Jade blew him a kiss. She stood at the door until the car turned the corner and was out of sight. She was grateful that Darrell had offered to pick up their son. It gave her the quiet time she needed to get that answer started – and hopefully completed! – So she could enjoy the weekend.

She leaned against the door after closing it. *It's funny how time changes so much,* she thought. *Places, music, fashion, hairstyles... and yet time can't change my feelings for Darrell.* She still loved him even more now than ever before.

She closed her eyes tightly and tried to push the thought of Darrell from her mind. For the life of her she couldn't understand how or why he continued to creep into her thoughts and dreams.

Jade moved from the door, realizing that just being here was probably part of her problem. Living in Darrell's house caused her to fantasize about the impossible. Marriage, more children, family vacations, late night... *Stop, it Jade*, she told herself. *Back to reality, girl. The only reason you're here is because you're the mother of his only child.*

That night when her place had been broken into – for the second time – Darrell had talked her into moving into his house. "The backyard is huge, Jade," he'd said persuasively. "And the neighborhood is great for raising kids. He's getting to the age where he needs the space to play and just be a little boy." He looked at Jade with the puppy-dog eyes that had always made her feel weak, and she was won over. Just thinking about his eyes made her... *Lord, you've got to help me. I'm reacting to his smile and the innocent touch of his hand and it's only a memory.*

Jade sat on the edge of her bed and picked up her book. A sheet of paper protruded from the book and she pulled it out. "That dang-gone list," she murmured to herself.

Over the last few months, as part of his campaign to get her to marry him, Darrell and Jade had discussed at length the kind of wife he should have. He thought Jade was perfect; she, on the other hand, wanted much more for him than she felt she could give.

Her finger traveled over the list she had made. She knew that most of the things she felt he needed were not a part of her makeup.

One: A virtuous woman.

Two: Strong family background.

Three: Educated.

She laughed at that one, because she knew she was nobody's dummy. She put a checkmark by number three.

Four: Strong relationship with the Lord.

She had been working on that one ever since Desmond came into her life. However, she still couldn't place a checkmark there – yet.

Five: Saved, sanctified, and speaking in tongues.

Well, she was saved, but she certainly wasn't sanctified and she didn't speak in tongues.

Jade shook her head, balled the paper up and tossed it into the wastebasket beside her nightstand. She didn't want to read the rest of it.

"Forget that list," she said out loud.

Why had she made it, anyway? It only reconfirmed all her imperfections! *Virtuous, sanctified, and speaking in tongues, that's a laugh.* And she knew that she didn't have a very strong family background.

Jade sniffed and looked around the room. She hated being alone. Not only was she alone, but she was also lonely. She despised living in Darrell's house. Being here forced her to constantly keep her guard up, protecting her innermost feelings. She couldn't allow what she really felt for Darrell to show, and she certainly couldn't allow him to get any deeper into her heart than he already was.

How in the world did I allow him to convince me to move in here in the first place? Jade laid back on her bed, staring at the ceiling. *No: it's not even my bed, it's his bed, and this is his room, his furniture, his everything.* Her past had led her irrevocably, it seemed, right here to this place, this time.

Jade and Darrell had met when classes resumed one fall at Camden High School. Jade was a junior and Darrell a senior. Her family had moved from Rocky Mount, North Carolina to Camden, New Jersey, six weeks before school started. Jade had been Darrell's first real girlfriend. Darrell entered Drexel University after graduating high school. One year later, Jade started attending Temple University. Their relationship grew and they were virtually inseparable. Everyone thought they would marry after Jade completed her undergraduate work.

However, it was Jade who decided to go on to law school, putting marriage off another three years. After completing the first year of law school, she packed up and moved to Maryland, baffling all her friends… and taking with her the secret of her pregnancy.

Jade contacted a temp agency and soon after they found her a job as a paralegal in Baltimore.

It wasn't long before Jade found her medical bills mounting. Temp agencies have no health benefits. A coworker told her to apply to the board of Social Services for help; and, having no other alternatives, Jade finally did so. She was approved to receive Medicaid, which paid for her medical care during her pregnancy.

Jade worked up until two days before delivering her son. The firm she worked for gave her three months to return to work. They were upfront and honest with her: they wanted her back. She was the best paralegal they had had in years, and it was no surprise that when she came back from her maternity leave, they offered her a full-time position.

Desmond was born on April first, and for the three months that Jade was out of work she received a welfare check from social services, who also helped her secure childcare so she could return to work. Jade accepted the full-time position offered by her law firm; it provided a salary of twenty-eight thousand a year and benefits.

Jade had just begun to build a new life for her and Desmond when Darrell found them. *That was certainly a trying time!* Jade remembered how angry Darrell was with her for not telling him about their son. Only Jade's parents and three closest friends knew she was pregnant, though she never admitted to Darrell being the father. Jade had told everyone the same thing she had put on the birth certificate: "Father Unknown."

Once Darrell found her and the truth about Desmond's paternity was in the open he – along with her friends – persuaded her to return to New Jersey and complete law school.

Jade remembered how Ivy Jones-Miller had gathered her three best friends together at her house, giving each one an envelope on which she had hand-written their names: Jade Sanders, Sheena Daniels, and Miranda Jones. They were put off for a moment when they found Ivy was giving them money.

Jade remembered thinking, *is this real? Her deceased husband must have left her loaded.* "Well, I'm so glad you're doing this," Jade had said happily. "Now I can put a nice down payment on a house and …"

"… move your behind back to Jersey," Ivy completed her sentence.

"What?"

"You can move back home. This fall I want you back in law school. If you run out of money before you finish, come see me. I need attorneys to watch my attorneys," Ivy said, laughing. "So you can pack your stuff and move your behind back home. Dee needs a father and I need my godson."

Sheena snickered at Jade.

"Oh, you find this humorous?" she snapped.

"Very much so. The money she gave me is a bribe *and* a wedding gift."

Jade smiled at the memory. Sheena was still single, so the bribe apparently hadn't worked.

Ivy was the widow of Raymond Miller, a professional football player who lost his life in a car accident, leaving Ivy with more money than she could spend in her lifetime. And Jade had to admit that she really did want to continue with her career, not just be a paralegal forever. Ivy was making that possible; her friend was giving her a future.

I should have put my furniture in storage, Jade admonished herself now. Before moving back, she had sold everything except her personal belongings; she had every intention of living with her mother. But after a week together, she realized that was impossible. Two grown women living in the same house didn't work at all. Staring at the ceiling, her mind went back to the conversation she had with her mother on last evening *chez* Nora Sanders.

"Jade Marie Sanders, are you listening to me?"

"Yes, Mom, I hear you."

Her mother was standing directly over her as Jade sat on her bed. Nora rarely gave her opinion, so Jade felt obligated to listen to her perception of what her daughter should do with her life. "What you need to do is marry that baby's daddy, and you should do it now. Enough of these ideas about you not being good enough for this man! Enough, do I make myself clear?"

"Perfectly." *But marrying Darrell would be both selfish and evil,* she thought.

Nora sat next to her daughter when she saw her drop her head and twist the ring on her finger. She placed a hand on her shoulder. "Jade, baby, what's wrong?" Jade looked down at the floor, unable to meet her mother's gaze. "I'll be the first to say that if you don't love this man, then by all means, walk away! But I know that's not the case. You love Darrell, Jade! I know it and you know it."

"Mama, Darrell wants things that I can't give him."

"There were things I couldn't give your father, but he loved me anyway."

There was a pause as they both thought about him; Jade's father had passed away almost two years before from a massive heart attack. She touched her mother's shoulder.

"Your father, Oh Lord, I loved your father."

"I know, Mama."

"He left me in a pickle. But I'm sure God... will..." her voice trailed off.

Jade wondered what pickle she was talking about. It wasn't the first time she heard her mother use that statement.

Nora straightened her spine and looked at Jade unwaveringly. "Name three things you can't give him, three reasons why you shouldn't marry him?"

"Well, for one, he wants a virtuous woman, and you and I know the real deal on that. Number two, he wants more children, and I never want to have another child: the baby factory is closed, thank you very much. And number three, I don't want..."

"Jade!" Jade's fourteen-year-old sister burst into the room to greet her.

"Hey, Theashia." Jade hugged her and kissed the girl's cheek.

"I didn't know you would be here today!"

"I didn't either. Mama wanted to talk to me about Darrell."

"Darrell." They said the name at the same time. "So when are you going to stop all the madness and let Darrell make an honest woman out of you?"

"Out of the mouth of babes." Nora tossed her oldest daughter a look.

"Seems to me both of you need to mind your own business." Jade frowned at her mother.

"You *are* my business," Nora said without missing a beat. "I only want to see you happy."

"I *am* happy." Jade said with a smile. "In just a few months I'll be graduating from law school. I already have a job offer and I'm…"

"You have a job offer?" Nora interrupted.

"Yes, I do."

"Where… who…?"

"Just last week I received a letter offering me a position from a firm called Jefferson and Mann."

"That's great, Jade," Theashia exclaimed with excitement. "Now you can buy me that new Xbox I want!"

Nora frowned. "Go to your room, young lady, and let the grown folks talk."

"I knew that was comin'."

"Bye, Ashia." Jade waved to her.

"I want to talk to you before you leave, okay?" Theashia lingered in the doorway.

"I'll be sure and stop by your room before I go," Jade assured her.

Theashia smiled and closed the door.

Jade looked at her mother. "Do I really need to tell you what number three is?"

Now the phone interrupted Jade's memory. She sighed, flipped over on the bed, and reached for the receiver. "Hello?"

"Hi, Jade. It's Pastor Owens."

"Hi, Pastor."

"I apologize for calling you so late. But I'm leaving early tomorrow morning for a conference and I'll be gone for a week."

"Oh, that's okay. What can I do for you?"

"We've had seven more kids register for math tutoring and I know you told me you didn't want any more students in your class, but I think I've come up with a solution: have two classes."

"That's sounds like a good idea. Who do you have to teach the other class?"

There was a long pause. Jade wondered if they had been disconnected. "Pastor Owens, are you still…."

"You, Jade," he answered finally.

Jade was silent. *He didn't just say* me, *did he?* "I can't teach two classes at the same time, Pastor."

"Well, they won't be at the same time. You'll teach the class you have now, just a half hour earlier, for one hour. Then you'll have a fifteen-minute break, and then you'll start the second class."

"I can't do that!" she protested. "I'm having problems making it on time as it is. Now you want me to start a half-hour earlier? I can't do it."

"Jade, I'll triple your fee. You're the best thing that's ever happened to these kids. They rave about you."

"Pastor, I can't do it. I have a full load and I have to study for my own classes."

"Please, Jade. Just pray about it. The parents enrolling their children are specifically asking for you."

Isn't he listening to me? "Pastor, I told you I couldn't take any more students. I'm at my limit."

"You don't realize the difference you're making, do you?"

"And I'm glad about that. It's just…"

"The kids that you've tutored say that their grades have risen from Ds to Bs. A few of your students are making As. Each time we get a new enrollment, they want you, and only you, as their child's tutor."

"Pastor, God knows I'm already stretching it."

"Jade, I know that you graduate from law school in just a few months. However, I really think your calling is in teaching. Teaching is a gift and you have a natural talent for it."

"Pastor…"

"You've been tutoring since you were in high school." There was a silent pause. "Now, I know that the teaching profession may not be as lucrative as becoming an attorney, but I think teaching is your passion as well as your calling."

This is sounding a little like blackmail, she thought. "Pastor, I only participated in this program to help some of the kids who told me they had problems with mathematics. I never expected it to go this far. This was never meant to become my career."

"I know that. But what I want you to do for me is meet with the parents on tomorrow morning."

"You've got to be joking! All I have to myself are my Saturdays, it's the only time I can take care of my personal business and…"

"Jade, it's only one Saturday morning. We had a church meeting last evening, and most of the meeting was about you."

"Look, I'm sure that the parents are grateful that their children are doing so much better. But I can't add…"

"Jade, you do remember James Johnson, don't you?"

She sighed. She knew what was coming. "Yes, of course I do."

"You do remember that he was labeled perceptually impaired, and the school system wanted to place him in a special school? Taking the short bus?"

"Pastor…"

"Look at him today, Jade. It was you that said he simply learns in a different way. You are the one that figured out how to reach him so he could learn. You know he took the SATs last month and scored a 975."

"What?"

"His mother was at the meeting. She came with her son and brought the report with her. You should have seen the gleam in that kid's eyes! And do you know who he gave credit to?"

"God?"

Pastor Owens laughed. "Well, he should have given the credit to God! However, he gave it to you. He stood up and told the church that if it had not been for Jade Sanders, he wouldn't have tried to get into college. He said that you took the time to teach him and you never made him feel like he was stupid."

"Well, that's because he's nowhere near stupid."

"Jade, as a favor to me, just get together with the parents tomorrow. Be at the church at ten o'clock in the morning. Hear them out and then when I get back you and I will meet and discuss your decision."

"You're twisting my arm, Pastor Owens." *And it doesn't feel good to get railroaded into this.*

"Well, maybe just a little. But you'll meet with them, right?"

Jade paused a long moment before giving in. "I'll be there."

CHAPTER TWO

The next day, immediately after the meeting at Pastor Owens' church, Jade went to the Parker's home to pick up her son.

Darrell's mother, Sonja Parker, met her at the door. "Jade, don't take him home right now, okay? Darrell just took him outside to play for a while."

"Well, I guess I could come back later... or maybe Darrell can drop him off."

"You don't have to leave. Stay here and visit with me for a bit. Would you like some iced tea?"

"No, thanks, Mrs. Parker." Jade was watching Darrell, who was now swinging Desmond around as the boy giggled uncontrollably.

Jade liked watching them together. Though Darrell had missed the first eighteen months of Dee's life, he had definitely made up for the lost time.

Jade had originally had no intention of telling Darrell about Desmond until the baby was much older. However, a mutual friend from college had seen Jade and Desmond together. The child's resemblance to his father made the relationship between the two unquestionable. The friend immediately contacted Darrell, who hired a private investigator to find them.

Jade took a sharp intake of breath when she saw Darrell toss Desmond in the air. The boy laughed aloud, asking his father to do it again. Desmond loved his father, there was no doubt about that; and Darrell's parents had spoiled the child rotten – as many grandparents do.

Jade stood there, her mind centered on Darrell. If things were different, she would have married him a year before Desmond was born. The boy's father was intelligent, kind, and drop-dead gorgeous. *Why am I standing here gazing at this man like he was a large double scoop of chocolate ice cream on a hot summer day? Why indeed? It's January.* She dropped her head and shut her eyes tightly. *I shouldn't even be here. Get away from the door and stop staring at the man, silly woman.*

Still standing at the patio door, Jade began praying. *Lord have mercy, and please lead me not into temptation. I'm truly trying to be holy.* A Scripture passage came to her mind: *Present your body as a living sacrifice, holy... holy... holy.* At that very moment Darrell waved, smiled and winked at her, and her heart skipped two beats as she waved back at him. *Oh, it is definitely time to leave.*

She turned to walk away and her eyes met his mother's. Jade knew from the smile on Mrs. Parker's face that she had been watching as Jade ogled her son. She couldn't look the woman in the eye for very long. Dropping her head, she thanked God Mrs. Parker couldn't read her thoughts.

"They're really enjoying themselves out there," Darrell's mother commented.

"Yes, they most certainly are. But I think it's much too cold for Dee." Jade walked over to the counter and leaned on it, glancing toward the patio doors, thinking – and even wishing – things could be different for them.

Darrell held down a full-time job at Waters Engineering firm, and he was working on his doctoral degree in theology. He didn't have the time to go to the gym like he used to. Nevertheless, Jade knew that hiding under the jacket was a muscular sculpture designed by heredity. *Lord help my mind*, she thought as she watched Darrell chase their three-year-old son around his parents' backyard. Bodybuilders worked hours to achieve the result that God gave him naturally. And, he's saved. So, who in their right mind wouldn't want to be with this man?

"Did you hear me, Jade?"

"Excuse me." Jade turned. "I'm sorry, Mrs. Parker, what did you say?"

"Come here, sweetie," Mrs. Parker pointed to the chair across from hers at the table in her large eat-in kitchen. "Let me talk to you for a minute."

Jade moved suspiciously to the table and sat down slowly.

"I understand that you don't want to attend Darrell's trial sermon. Is there any reason why?"

"I just rather not be there, that's all."

"But you must have a reason why you feel you shouldn't," Sonja prodded.

"I guess it's for the same reason I moved my membership to Greater Mt. Carmel."

"That's another thing. I never understood why you left the church you've been a member of since you were a child."

Once again Jade wished she had been a different person or born to a different family. Maybe then she and Darrell wouldn't be in the predicament in which they found themselves. She was doing all she could to straighten out her life. She had recommitted her life to the Lord, and had remained celibate since before Desmond was born. But God knows it hadn't been easy.

"Well, it's because everyone at Cathedral of Faith know me, and… well, they know Darrell… and every time they see us together, they speculate about our relationship. I know Darrell doesn't need that right now. He needs to stay focused, and I don't want my presence to cause a distraction."

"I think your *not* being there will be more of a distraction than you being there."

"Mrs. Parker, I've heard what the people at Cathedral say about me. I know they think that I am to Darrell as Delilah was to Samson."

The older woman pursed her lips. "That's all on you, child. That's goin' on in your head, not out here in the real world. No one but you is sayin' that kind of nonsense." She chuckled.

Jade didn't see the humor. "Well actually, I've heard worse, but I respect you too much to repeat it."

"Jade, it shouldn't matter what people think about you. It only should matter what the Lord knows about you." Mrs. Parker leaned back in her chair as she appraised Jade. "Do you realize that you are not the same person you were when you first came back here to live? Baby, you're not even the same person you were six months ago, for that matter." She placed her hand on Jade's. "I've watched you grow spiritually over the months. And I know that only God could make the changes I see in you." She smiled, and Jade smiled in return. "And I know you love my son as much as he loves you." It was true, she loved Darrell probably more than he loved her, so how could she protest? "I see the way you look at him and he looks at you."

"Mrs. Parker…"

"Hush, child, and let me say my piece."

"Yes, ma'am."

"I've been watchin' you two. And it's dangerous for you and him to have what I see in your eyes for each other and not be in a position to do anything about it."

Oh, Lord, how in the world can she see my very thoughts through my eyes? Jade dropped her head.

"You and Darrell need to marry and give that boy out there a normal life. Holy matrimony is the only thing you all can do. It's what you *need* to do."

"Mrs. Parker, I don't think your husband would agree with you."

"My husband is old, judgmental and set in his ways."

"But like him, I want…"

"This is not about what you want, young lady. So stop being selfish." She picked up her iced tea and took a sip. "Tell my son yes the next time he asks you to marry him."

Selfish? Jade thought, her mouth agape. *I've sacrificed my happiness to be sure Darrell's place in the ministry is not jeopardized because of me, and I'm being selfish?* Jade wanted to rebuke her; but then she heard a gentle voice within her say, *not a word.* She closed her mouth and stared into space. There was a long period of silence.

"I overheard him talking to his father the other day. He told him he was going to keep asking until you said yes. So that's where things stand, and I'm not sayin' anything more. Now that I've said my piece about that, I want to know about the meeting you had this morning at Pastor Owens' church."

"Oh, well, I met with the parents of all my students this morning."

"All of them? Good heavens!"

"Every one of them was there. They're talking about the church starting its own school and they asked if I would consider a position as principal or headmistress."

"They're goin' start a private school?"

"I don't know. But I do know they are seriously discussing it."

Mrs. Parker shook her head. "Well, God knows you've made an great impact on their after-school program."

"So they say."

"No. Look at me. You really have, Jade."

"Well, I'm glad I could help." She shrugged. "But, anyway, I explained to them that I couldn't consider it. I don't want to teach, I want to practice law. But I've decided to continue with the tutoring program for four more months and I'm going to take on a second class as well."

"Another class, that's really gonna be hard on you. I mean with you trying to study for your own classes."

"I know, but after I heard a few praise reports, I couldn't resist helping a few more kids." *Yep,* she thought, *I really did let them talk me into it.*

"Well, you've always had that teaching nature in you. You've been tutoring kids since you were a kid."

Jade smiled. "So I've been told."

"You know, Jade, I've truly grown to admire you." Jade was shocked to hear her words. "I see why my son is so in love with you." Sonja stood up, patted Jade's hand and went to the stove to stir her pot.

"Mrs. Parker, you are right about what you said earlier. I do love Darrell."

Mrs. Parker stopped stirring, placed her hand on her hip and turned toward Jade. "You say you love him, but your actions show something different."

Jade dropped her head, wondering if she should tell Darrell's mother the truth so she would stop pushing her into her son's life. *You don't have to reveal everything*, she told herself. *Just enough to let her know that Darrell should find himself a woman who is more suited for his life in the ministry.* Jade began twisting the ring on her finger.

"Jade." Mrs. Parker put her hand on top of Jade's, putting a halt to the twisting. "He doesn't want to be with anyone but you."

How does she do that? How does she know what I'm thinking? Jade drew strength from deep within herself. She wasn't one to show a lot of emotion and she decided to be as honest as she could with this woman. Maybe after she explained herself, Sonja would understand that not only was she not being selfish, but that she loved him enough to let him go even though she wanted him so.

Darrell's mother was still talking. "He told me and his daddy a good while back that if he could remove what was in his heart for you, he would, but that he couldn't. This whole thing has been hard on him, and I'm sure it can't be easy for you either. Forcing yourself to be separated from him this way. My fear is that temptation may get the best of you two in one way or another. It's already happened more than once, as we both know, and Desmond is proof of that."

"If I can, Mrs. Parker, I'd like to be blunt with you. What I'm about to say may even be disturbing, so I'm going to apologize now for what I'm about to say."

Sonja turned the fire off under her pot and came to sit at the table across from Jade. "Please go on."

"Darrell and I met when I was in the eleventh grade – as you well know. He was a senior. And, at the time, I never thought about who or what he would be in the future. I just knew he wasn't like other guys." Jade began to ramble a bit. "I knew he wasn't ordinary at all. And I… well, I ignored that and I did the unthinkable. I… I brought him down to my level."

"Jade, Darrell isn't a…"

"Please, you said what you needed to say! Now let me say what's in my heart!"

Sonja folded her arms. "Okay."

"Darrell is truly a man of God. And I knew that before I seduced him into my bed."

Darrell's mother's mouth dropped open and Jade didn't care to see *that look* on her face, so she stood up and walked to the door. As she watched Darrell pushing Dee, on a swing she prayed silently, *God, please help me say what needs to be said politely and with tact.*

"I know you remember that time you came to see Darrell on campus early on a Saturday morning and I was there."

"I remember. His father was so upset with you two."

"And he had every right to be. That's when it all started." Jade took a deep breath. "You and your husband gave that long lecture, and for the life of me I could never remember a word of it. For me it was in one ear and out the other. But Darrell, he was Godly sorry, and for a long time he wouldn't come near me. His dorm room was totally off limits, and we met in very public places with lots of people." Jade didn't want to, but she pressed on anyway. "I plotted against him. The first time I did it I… I truly didn't know what I was doing. I just knew what I wanted and… and I… I meant to get what I wanted. But with time, I became quite an expert at the art of seduction."

Sonja was looking at her in astonishment. "So are you saying to me that you forced yourself on my son?"

Jade thought about her question. Darrell had wanted to do what was morally correct. He wanted to wait until they were married before engaging in a sexual relationship. But Jade enjoyed sex too much to become celibate. It took months of fasting and praying to get her to that point.

"Jade…"

"That's exactly what I'm saying."

"Jade, you give yourself too much credit." She was almost chuckling. "Darrell may be called by God, but he's still a man! He wanted what you offered! My son is like his father. He just loves hard, that's all. I knew when we came to your house to take pictures for the prom that Darrell had fallen in love, and he had fallen hard, and that was long before that morning in his dorm room. Your mother and I talked a long time after the two of you left. I told her then that we may as well get ready for a wedding, because my son was crazy about you."

Jade was fascinated. "My mother never told me you said that."

"Well, maybe it's because she didn't want to think about losing her little girl! Jade, Darrell doesn't wear a halo, so don't put him on a pedestal."

"Mrs. Parker, I'm not what you think I am, either."

"Who is? Only God can see the innermost part of a person."

"I'm no good for your son, and I knew it almost from the beginning." Jade wiped at the mist in her eyes. "My mother told me to walk away before I got too emotionally attached. I should have listened to her. But back then, I *was* being very selfish." Jade sat back down at the table. "You see, I used Darrell to try and fill an emptiness that was inside of me. I didn't understand things the way I do now. I should never have allowed myself to get involved with him."

Jade looked down at her hands as she twisted her ring, wondering how much to tell Darrell's mother. "But I'm not being selfish now, and I'm not being selfish anymore. I want only the very best for him. If I thought I was the best for him, I would marry him in a heartbeat."

"You're much too hard on yourself, my dear."

Oh God I don't want to tell her. "Dee wasn't an accident, Mrs. Parker."

"What?"

"I knew that I was going to lose Darrell to the ministry and I wanted to keep a part of him with me." The shock on Mrs. Parker's face made Jade lose control of the tears she had been holding back. "Mrs. Parker, I can't erase what I did in the past. But I can certainly control my actions now, and I refuse to bring him down to my level ever again. Darrell has a prophetic ministry and I want him to be the man God intends him to be. I won't be his Delilah and I won't... I will *not* be the one to destroy him."

Mrs. Parker leaned back in her chair. Jade could tell she didn't know what to say. Fortunately, Dee chose that moment to burst into the house. "Grandma, Grandma!" He rushed to his grandmother and she stretched her arms out for a hug. "Oh, goodness, you're freezing! Darrell, you know better than to have him out in the cold air that long!"

"He wanted to stay out," Darrell answered, casually taking a banana from the fruit bowl on the counter.

"Me and Daddy's gonna go to Toy Land!"

Jade wiped her eyes in an effort to compose herself. "No, Dee, it's Daddy and I."

Dee nodded his head. "Daddy and me."

Jade threw up her hands and smiled, but she couldn't hide her tears from Darrell. He peeled his banana, moving closer to her before responding. "Don't worry about that. He'll get it right. The boy's only three."

Mrs. Parker put both her hands on Dee's cheeks. "His face is frozen."

"I had him wrapped up." Looking at his son, he asked, "You cold?"

Dee shook his head. "Nope."

"You ready to go, little man?" Darrell asked his son.

"Uh-huh. Come on, Mommy! Git'cha coat!" Dee raced from the room.

"Come on Mommy, git'cha coat. Darrell mimicked his son as he used his hand to beckon Jade to followed behind him.

Jade stood up to leave and Mrs. Parker caught her by the arm. "God is the only one to give life," she said, "accident or not."

ೞೞಚಚ

When Darrell brought them home from Toy Land, he stayed around the house to give Dee a bath. After he tucked him in for the night, he found Jade curled up on the sofa in the family room watching television.

"Hey, I thought you were going to study for a while."

"I know. But I decided to watch this movie instead. I needed to relax my mind."

Darrell sat next to her, lifting her legs and placing her feet on his lap.

Jade really wasn't watching the movie. She had been thinking about her maternal grandmother who had been a part of her life up until she was ten years old. She had loved her Grand Matilda and never understood why God took her away from her.

Darrell was massaging her feet. She closed her eyes tightly enjoying his magical hands and wondering what Grand Matilda would think about this man. Matilda wasn't a saint. She ran a liquor house and Jade never ever remember her stepping foot in a church. She was known as the root woman and people from miles around would come see her. Jade never knew what she did or how she did it.

Darrell said something interrupting her thoughts. "...at the house."

"I'm sorry, what did you say?"

His eyes were on the television screen as he repeated. "Did my mother say something to upset you at the house?"

"No, not at all," Jade answered slowly.

"Then why were you crying?" He still wasn't looking at her, giving her some space.

"That's between your mother and me." Jade was terse.

"Look, I know my mother." He shifted so he could look at her. "She thinks she can say whatever she wants to people, because as she says, she's at that age where she can be brutally honest, and I..."

"Your mother didn't say or do anything to me, okay?"

Darrell gazed at her for a moment. "Okay."

Jade moved her eyes back to the television screen.

"Since we're sitting here like this can we talk?"

Here we go again. "What do you want to talk about, Darrell?"

"Anything, tell me something about your childhood."

"Like what?"

"Anything."

Jade looked at him for a moment. "I was close to my grandmother. I miss her. I miss her a lot." She said softly.

"How old were you when she died?"

"Ten." Just remembering that time made Jade's heart ache.

"I remember my grandfather use to take me fishing. I always liked that. What do you remember most about your grandmother?"

Fishing? Oh, please, Jade thought. *No cursing and gambling? Dancing... no grinding to the music while dancing in the living room of his home? No... that never ever would have happened in his neat little world.* Something in Jade snapped. "I remember she was a voodoo priestess." She pulled herself away from him and stood up. "So let's just drop it." Using the remote, she clicked off the television. "I'm tired, Darrell. I don't want to talk. I'm going to bed." She left the room quickly, knowing it was the best thing to do. Sitting there with her feet in his lap was totally improper.

Darrell blew out a long sigh watching her as she switched out of the room. He just couldn't understand her. Just when he thought she was about to open up, she says something sarcastic like voodoo and leave the room. Why did he allow this woman to continue treating him so arrogantly? He needed to do what Jason had done with Sheena: just walk away. That had been a bold move on Jason's part, giving up the fight and leaving the woman he loved.

The reality was that Darrell just couldn't find it in his heart to do the same. On top of his feelings for her, he and Jade shared a son – Jason only had himself to worry about. Darrell knew that pressing Jade tonight was out of the question. He'd have to find out what had made her cry another day. So he walked out of the house, locking the door behind him.

Jade stood at the bedroom window, watching Darrell get into his car. The telephone rang and she answered it, still watching the car pull out of the driveway.

"Hello?" Her voice was barely above a whisper.

"Yes, hello. I'm looking for Jade. Jade Sanders."

The voice was not familiar. "Who's calling?"

"I'm an old friend of hers."

She still hadn't recognized the voice. "An old friend?"

"Is this Jade?"

"Yeah," she answered without thinking. "Who is this?"

"Oh, thank God, I found you. This is Keith. Keith Strickland."

She asked the question even though she knew exactly who he was before she asked again. "Who is this?"

"It's Keith, Jade. I've been looking for you for months."

Jade felt faint. "For what? I mean, why?"

"I need any information you can give me about the adoption of our child."

CHAPTER THREE

Jade barely slept after talking to Keith Strickland that night.

She got up earlier than usual, called her mother, and then called Darrell, asking him if she could bring Desmond to spend the day with him. After dropping the boy off she headed straight to her mother's house.

"Hi, Mom." Jade kissed her mother's cheek as soon as she opened her front door. "Where's Theashia?" She removed her coat.

"I dropped her off at the church for Sunday school."

Jade walked into the living room with her mother following behind her. "What's going on?" the older woman asked.

Jade sat in the chair next to the window and began twisting the ring on her finger, a sure sign she was upset. "Why are you so nervous?" Even over the phone Nora could tell something or someone had disturbed her. "Jade," Nora touched her daughter's shoulder and Jade looked at her with tears in her eyes. "Baby, what's wrong?"

"Keith called me."

"Keith?"

"Keith Strickland, Mom." She was almost shouting.

At first her mother was clueless; then, slowly, she remembered. "Keith Strickland from Rocky Mount, North Carolina," she said, nodding. Her recognition was followed immediately by alarm. "He called you at home? You mean at Darrell's house?"

"Can you believe that?"

"How did he get the number? What did he want?" Nora walked closer to Jade and stood over her, as though by her very physical presence she could protect her daughter.

"He wanted information about the adoption."

Nora stroked Jade's arm in an effort to comfort her. "Why? I mean… why now, after all these years?"

"I don't know. I told him I couldn't give him any information. He told me that he would find out, with or without my help. He said it's been haunting him for years."

"Oh, God, what else did he say?" Nora sat down in a chair across from Jade, frowning, her mind racing.

"Well, the first thing I asked him was how he found me. And then, he told me."

♋♓

Keith's voice was strong in her ear. "I started with the Division of Motor Vehicles. They had an old address in Camden. But when I went to that address, the woman next door told me you moved more than a year ago. She said I could probably find you through the college. She's the one that told me you were a law student at Rutgers. So, that's how I found you."

"Someone at the school gave you my *personal* information?" Jade's fear made her strident.

"No, of course not. But I talked to a lot of people. One of your classmates told me you lived in Medford with a guy name Darrell Parker. I found him on the Internet along with his address and phone number."

"Who was it that told you?" She knew she was asking irrelevant questions. *Anything not to have to face what he really has to say.*

"I gave my word I wouldn't tell where I got the information."

She took a deep breath, steadying herself. "What do you want, Keith?"

"I'd like to meet with you if I can."

"For what? We said all we needed to say to each other years ago." Jade paused. "Why, Keith? Why after all this time? You never cared."

"That's not true."

"You never fought to keep the baby. You left me alone. You allowed your family to belittle me and it hurt."

"I was a kid, Jade!"

"Well, so was I." She wanted to scream and controlled herself with some effort. She couldn't risk waking Dee. "I was younger than you. But *I* still had to deal with it."

"I was wrong. I'm sorry."

"Yes, you *are* sorry." She was being mean and she didn't care. How dare he?

He reacted to the sharpness in her voice. "Well, I guess you weren't any better than I was. *You* allowed our child to be adopted!"

"What was I supposed to do? I didn't have a job. I couldn't take care of any baby. And the daddy wasn't exactly there to help. What did you expect me to do?"

Jade drew in another deep breath. "You really have some nerve calling me and asking me about –"

He interrupted her. "What agency handled the adoption?"

"I'm not giving you any information. I'm not going to allow you to disrupt another person's life."

A pause. "You're not the least bit curious about the child, Jade?"

"No. I don't have the right to be curious. I gave up my rights and so did you when we signed to give that child away."

"I understand you have a son now."

"Keith, I don't care to discuss my personal affairs with you. Please don't call here again."

"Wait, Jade! Don't hang up. Just tell me… Why are you so hostile?"

"I'm not hostile. Listen to me carefully. I want nothing to do with you. I don't want any kind of communication with you. Not by phone, snail mail, email, telegram, or any other means you might dream up. Do I make myself clear?"

"Perfectly."

"Good. You have a nice life." *Click.*

හ
ආලි

"That's the whole conversation, Mama."

"Well, I guess I'll have to make a few phone calls," Nora sighed.

Jade turned to her, feeling very much like a child again herself. "I'm scared! I don't want Darrell to know about this. I don't want *anybody* to know!"

"I'm going to take care of it, baby." Nora tried to console her daughter. "Don't you worry, 'cause I don't want those records opened any more than you do." She pulled Jade into a firm embrace.

"So, what are you going to do?"

"I'm going to get some expert advice. In the meantime, I don't want you to worry about it. You just concentrate on finishing school."

৵৩

The next few days were ordinary enough to make that night's conversation feel like a dream. Jade had not heard anything from Keith Strickland and she counted it a blessing. By the end of the week, she had easily merged back into her busy schedule as mommy, student and tutor.

On Friday, Jade went to Taco Palace to meet her best friends for dinner.

Ivy was eager to hear about school. "Were you able to register for all the classes you needed?"

"Yes, but only because I took those two classes during summer semester," Jade answered. Ivy had agreed with Darrell that Jade should relax for the summer; but Jade had studied instead, acing both classes. "I'm so glad this is my last semester. In four more months, this whole odyssey will be over!"

Ivy dipped a chip in salsa several times. "Well, I still say, all work and no play makes Jade a moody woman." She popped the chip into her mouth.

"You of all people know I have to finish school this year! I don't have time to play around."

"And I must say you've been true to your convictions. But now that you're on the last lap, you need to start thinking about life after the bar exam."

Jade tilted her head to one side, considering what to say. She and Ivy had been friends for over seventeen years, and she knew that Ivy's concern was genuine. Ivy knew a lot about rebuilding after loss. "I've been making plans for the future," Jade said.

"Uh-huh."

Jade searched desperately for a change of subject. "So tell me how the decorating's coming along in the new house?"

Ivy's eyes lit up. "Girl, I'm having the time of my life! The whole inside is done and I'm almost finished with the garden. It's so beautiful, Jade! I really think it's going to be my sanctuary."

"The whole house is a sanctuary. You've built yourself a mansion."

"I wouldn't call it a mansion. It's just a large home."

"Uh-huh, and ice ain't cold."

Ivy narrowed her eyes. "But this isn't about me. You know, you always do that."

"Do what?"

"Change the subject on me. How did we start talking about my house when we were talking about you, Ms. Thing?"

Jade sipped her water. "I know what you're leading up to, Ivy Jones-Miller, and I'm not debating with you today." She rolled her eyes. "I'm not in the mood."

"Well, Ms. Jade Marie Sanders, I'm just looking out for my godson. You know that short, little, curly-head guy with the gray eyes, who Christian name is Desmond? The one everyone calls Dee?"

"See, that's what you don't understand. I'm looking out for the welfare of my son and his future. Why do you think I came back here in the first place? I'll tell you why. It's because of Dee, not me. I want what's best for him." Jade felt her temper flaring. "That's why I'm thinking of moving to Tampa once I finish school."

"Tampa? You mean the one in Florida? Pass me that white sauce."

Jade laughed. "Yes," she said and pushed the saucer over to Ivy. "Tampa, Florida. The Jefferson and Mann Law Firm came on campus just before Christmas scouting for potential associates and they asked to see me."

"They asked to see *you*?"

"Yes, Ivy, they wanted to see me. I haven't been looking for a job. The only thing I'd been concentrating on is trying to make good grades." Ivy continued to stare at Jade suspiciously. "I'm telling you the truth."

"So why didn't you tell me about it when they first talked to you?"

"I really didn't think anything of it. I certainly never thought they'd offer me a position before I graduated."

Ivy almost choked on her water with lemon. "They offered you a job?"

"Yes, and the offer stand as long as I graduate with a 3.4 G.P.A."

Ivy snickered. "Well, you can just forget that, 'cause Darrell Parker Jr. is not going to let you take his son out of this state."

Jade knew she was right.

"Here." Ivy pushed the basket of chips in front of her. "Have some corn chips."

"No, thanks. I just want some food."

Ivy folded her hands in front of her on the table. "So, go on."

"I'm really considering it. I need to leave this area. I want a chance to build my own life without leaning on my friends and my baby's daddy."

"You can do that right here, Ms. Thing."

"Darrell will never let me do that. He thinks we should be together."

"He's not the only one who thinks that. Everyone who knows the two of you thinks that."

"Well, we don't have a future together. We share one thing, and that's Dee. If I didn't have him, I would never have come back here."

"If you hadn't had Dee you probably wouldn't have left here in the first place, and maybe you and Darrell wouldn't have broken up in the first place and maybe, just maybe, you wouldn't feel like you aren't worthy enough to marry him."

"That's crazy."

"Think so?"

"I know so."

"Well, I think I've figured something out about you." Ivy tilted her head and considered her friend. "You have low self-esteem."

"No, that's…"

Ivy held up her hand to stop Jade's rebuttal. "Wait a minute. Don't shake your head like that. Just hear me out." Ivy paused a moment to get her thoughts together. She'd been waiting for an opportunity to say this to her friend, but she didn't want it to come out wrong and offend her. Ivy reached across the table and grasped both of Jade's hands. "I've been watching you, I mean really watching you, since you've been back home. You keep saying that Darrell needs to find a woman who's… what's the word you used… wholesome? It's like you've labeled yourself unworthy of being with him, and it's all because you got pregnant out of wedlock."

Jade pulled her hands away from Ivy's and leaned back in her chair.

Ivy pressed on. "What you need to realize is that you didn't get pregnant all by yourself. That would have been one major miracle! Darrell was there with you.

He's the child's father. I mean… you didn't *rape* the man, for goodness sake!" Ivy sat back in her chair. "He without sin cast the first stone."

"I'm like Delilah to him. He's better off without me."

"Why do you think he's better off without you, Jade?"

"I influenced him. I'm the one that made our relationship what it was. He always wanted to wait. He told me that we should wait. But I wouldn't hear it. I provoked him."

"You can lead a horse to the water, girl, but you can't make him drink. Darrell did what he wanted to do."

"But I led him into temptation!"

"Temptation isn't a sin, Jade. Yielding to the temptation was the sin. He drank the water because he wanted to. Hell, Eve didn't make Adam eat the forbidden fruit. She just offered it to him. So stop beating yourself up!"

Jade thought about what Mrs. Parker told her. *Darrell may be called by God, but he's still a man."* I'll be able to do that when I'm far away from him."

"Oh, I see. You think being away from him is going to stop you from loving him?"

Jade stopped sipping her water and set her glass down in front of her, holding it with both hands. "It's my opinion that if Delilah had just left Samson alone, things could have been a whole lot different. I'm doing that for Darrell. I'm leaving the man of God alone. I'm doing something for him the devil will never do."

Someone pulled out a chair at the table and they both looked up. "Hey, did you all order for me?"

"No, but I was about to order without you." Ivy answered Miranda. "Where's Sheena? I thought you said she was with you."

Ivy and Jade looked toward the door.

"Who you looking for?" Sheena asked as she pulled out the fourth chair beside Jade.

Jade whipped her head around. "Where'd you come from?"

"You'd know the answer to that question if you and Ivy wasn't so deep in conversation."

"Looks like they were bickering at each other to me."

"No way! Besides, that's *my* job," Sheena replied with a grin.

"I'm not bickering, and I'm certainly not up to debating either," Jade responded, looking directly at Sheena.

Ivy was nonchalant. "As a matter of fact we *are* in a heavy debate."

"Ivy, please. Not right now."

"Oh, I have to know what's going on!" Miranda said. "Pass me them chips!"

The waiter walked over to their table. "Are you ladies ready for me to take your drink order?"

"I'm ready, 'cause I'm hungry," Miranda answered.

"You could have eaten a hour ago and you'd be hungry," Ivy said under her breath.

"What was that, mother hen?"

"Oh, nothing, will you just decide what you want?"

After they ordered, Miranda took a careful sip of water before speaking. "So what is it you don't want to talk about, Jade?"

Jade ignored Miranda. "What's this about you joining a commune, Sheena?"

"I'm not joining a commune. I just told Ivy that so mother hen would have some excuse for my mood the other day."

"You know what, you are a real trip, Sheena."

"Well, I had to tell you *something,* mommy dearest."

"Forget you, Sheena." Ivy turned to Jade. "So are you really thinking about moving to Tampa, or did you make that up for my benefit too?"

"No, I'm serious."

Sheena laughed out loud. "That idea is crazier than me joining a commune."

"Crazier than me losing one hundred pounds," Miranda added.

Jade shrugged. "Look, I have to graduate before I can even consider it."

"Stop it, Jade, you're already contemplating it," Ivy said, raising her voice.

Jade turned her head and stared out the window, silent and annoyed.

"Why didn't somebody order cheese sauce?" Miranda waved for the waiter. "I'm not worried 'bout her goin' nowhere, 'cause Jade knows Darrell ain't gonna let her take his son from him."

"*Si, Senorita?*"

"Can you get us some cheese dip, please?" The waiter nodded and left.

"Like I was telling Jade. She needs to get a new plan, 'cause that one's out of the question," Ivy commented.

All the girls agreed.

Jade knew it too. There was no way Darrell would accept her moving Dee that far away. But she knew she needed to get as far away from him as possible. They had settled into an excessively comfortable routine. Darrell supported her and their son financially. Darrell's parents lived about a half a mile away from his house and his mother was their babysitter. The arrangement was convenient and way too comfortable.

"Jade…" Jade looked at Miranda. "Where are you, girl? The man is trying to take your food order!"

"Yes, *please* let the man do his job so he can stop looking at me like I'm this week's special." Sheena was frowning.

"Oh. Sorry," mumbled Jade. "Just give me a number five, please."

"*Gracias*." The waiter walked away after turning his nose up at Sheena.

"Jeez, Sheena, you didn't have to talk to the man so nastily," Ivy commented.

"Yeah, he might get back there and do something to our food," added Miranda.

"That's right. I heard about this waiter who put urine in a customer's drink," Ivy said with a wicked smile.

"If you know about it then they must have caught him," Miranda remarked.

"Yeah, but not until after he took a few swallows." Ivy took a sip of water.

"Oh, now that's just nass and tee." Miranda put her hand over her eyes.

Sheena was barely listening to them. "Look, I'm tired of men looking at me like I don't have any clothes on. I'm not taking it anymore."

"Sheena, you're trippin'," Miranda said. "You know men are gonna be mesmerized by your beauty even if you don't want them to be."

"If it was Jason she wouldn't be trippin'." Ivy mumbled.

"What was that?" Sheena asked. Ivy ignored her.

"How's your mother doing Randi?"

"Thank God, she's still in remission. But please keep her in prayer. This cancer has come back twice so I'm hoping it won't show up anymore." Miranda emptied a pouch of sweetener in her iced tea. "Have you heard from Jason?"

Sheena paused and shook her head. "No. Not a thing."

"So that's why you've been in an ugly mood." Miranda stirred her tea. "Why don't you call him?" Ivy kicked Miranda under the table. "Hey! Ouch!"

Sheena needled her eyebrow before answering Miranda. "He doesn't *want* me to call him, that's why."

"How long has he been gone now?" Jade asked softly.

"Three months, two days and" – she looked at her watch – "two and a half hours."

Miranda bit into a chip. "If I were you, I'd give homeboy a visit."

"I can't do that."

"You know what, you and Jade's situation has really gotten old. Do you know how many women on this planet have been on bended knees begging God to send them a good man, but no: the two of you rather be alone. I don't get it," Miranda complained.

"Shut up, Rugrat," Ivy snapped.

"Did you find a new bowling partner to replace Jason yet?" Jade asked.

"Yeah, and that's the only good news I have to report."

"Well, who is it?" Ivy asked.

"It's one of the investigators at the office. You all don't know her."

"What's her name?" Miranda dipped a chip in sauce and flopped it in her mouth.

"Josephine Knight."

"Is she good?" Ivy asked.

"She's real good. I think she's better than Jason."

"Well, that's good. Maybe you can win the doubles this year," Ivy responded.

"Maybe," Sheena was somber.

After a brief silence Miranda announced, "Well, *I* have good news! I've met someone." She smiled as everyone looked at her. "His name is Kyle and he is *so* fine!"

All the other girls looked at each other. They had never heard Miranda talk about a man with such excitement.

"Well, well, well," said Ivy slowly. "A man has finally knocked you off your feet."

"I wouldn't say all that. But I do remember chastising myself when I first got a good look at him."

"Really? How did you meet him?"

"My car broke down in Philly, right on the Schuylkill Expressway. Here I was trying to get to work on time, and the stupid thing kept jerking and acting real crazy. Anyway, there was this BMW directly behind me, and I just knew he was teed off at me 'cause he almost ran into the back of me. I pulled over and he went around me and pulled over in front of my car. I can't lie: I got scared. But I told myself, *Okay, Miranda, be calm and stay in the car. The best thing to do is to be nice, no matter how nasty he gets. Oh, and don't forget to apologize for having this old beat-up 1994 Ford LTD on the road in the first place.*"

The girls laughed and Miranda joined them before continuing.

"As he came closer my mouth just *dropped*. The man is drop-dead *gorgeous*! Skin the color of pecan, and, good lord, he was tall! Every bit of six feet or more! And the suit he wore looked as if it was tailor-made to his body."

"Girl you were lusting! Did you repent?"

"Several times." They all laughed again.

"Listen to my baby cousin. All excited and stuff."

"Shut up, Ivy, let the woman tell her story." Jade scowled.

"Anyway, as he reached the side of my car he pushed his hands into his pockets, and bent down so he could speak to me through the crack in my window."

ᔕᗺᘓᘓ

"Hi, I see you're having a bit of trouble."

Breathe, Miranda, she said to herself. "Ahh yes," she stammered. "I am. This is the second time this week." *All right, so it's not the smartest thing in the world to say.* "I've had two different mechanics look at it. I – um – " *Get your hormones under control, girlfriend!* "I'm so sorry. I know I almost caused you to run into me."

"No, not really. I could tell something was wrong because your car kept jerking," he said, then smiled at her. She was almost ready to throw caution to the wind. Her eyes widened as she took a good look at him. The cleft in his chin made him look even more distinguished. *Ooh my God…* She was staring at him. She turned her head to look at the traffic ahead of her, trying to ignore the fact that she was totally captivated by this man. "I'm no mechanic," he continued, "but I have a friend that has a shop on Grays Ferry. I can get him to take a look at your car if you'd like."

"That's awfully nice of you, but putting another dime in this car is just throwing good money away. Besides, that's the least of my problems right now."

"Really? What other problems could a beautiful lady like you have?"

No. He did not say what he just said to me. Her knuckles paled as she gripped the steering wheel. Hard. *Okay, Miranda, here comes the pick-up line.* She took a deep breath and blew it out before saying, "Well, because of this, I probably won't get to work on time. And that means that after 8:30 this morning, I'll have no job."

"You'll get fired over not getting to work?"

"You can bet on it."

He looked at her for a moment before asking, "Who do you work for?"

She sighed. "Tri-State Engineering."

He tilted his head to one side and half-smiled. "Is your boss's name Chris Davis?"

"Yes! You know him?"

"Yeah, Chris and I go way back. We're good friends. Let me get my cell phone and I'll give him a call."

He walked away before Miranda could object. He reached inside his car and walked back to her with his phone in hand. "I'm sorry, I didn't get your name. I'm Kyle Waters and you are…?"

"Miranda Jones."

"Well, I'm pleased to meet you, Ms. Jones."

"Likewise, Mr. Waters." They both smiled foolishly at the formality of the words.

Kyle began to dial a number as he walked back toward his car. Miranda figured that whatever he was doing couldn't put her in any more hot water than she was already in right now.

After a time he walked back to her car and announced, "Chris wants to speak with you." She rolled her window down just enough to retrieve the phone from him. He laughed, clearly aware of the fact that she was being cautious of a stranger.

"Hello?"

"Hi, Miranda. Kyle just told me what was going on. He says he has a friend that can take a look at your car and he feels pretty confident that he can get you back on the road in no time."

"Well, he offered, but I don't think working on this car is a good idea."

"Miranda, you need transportation to get back and forth to work, don't you?"

"Yes, but…"

"Kyle is offering to help you, so if I were you, I'd accept his generosity."

"In all honesty, Mr. Davis, I don't feel comfortable having Mr. Waters go out of his way to help me."

"I can understand you being apprehensive about a stranger. He said you were talking to him through a small opening in your window."

Miranda sighed. "I don't know him, Mr. Davis."

"I totally understand and so does he. You have every right to be on your guard in a city like Philadelphia. However, Kyle is good people, Miranda. You don't have to be concerned about his intentions. He's highly regarded. " He paused a moment and Miranda took a deep breath and looked over at Kyle who was looking out at the passing cars. "Listen, why don't you take the day off and don't worry about anything pending at the office today. Whatever you have can wait. Let Kyle help you with your car and I'll see you tomorrow."

"Tomorrow?"

He sounded exasperated. "Miranda, by the time you take care of your car, the day will be gone. Now, let me speak with Kyle."

Without another word of protest, Miranda rolled the window down completely and gave the phone back to Kyle.

−•−

"So," Miranda concluded, "The Philadelphia City police arrived, and put some flares around my car. It took almost two hours for the tow truck to come and load the car and pull it away. But Kyle stayed with me the whole time. Then, he took me to his friend's shop and made him promise he'd fix my car! And not only that, he had the man loan me a car from his lot to drive while mine was being repaired!"

"Well, you'd really be telling me something if when you got the car back you had no bill." Sheena hoped that was the case.

Miranda smiled. "Exactly."

Ivy paused, her fork in front of her mouth. "Exactly? What do you mean? He paid the bill?" Jade gasped.

"Yes! I got my car and I had no bill." She stretched her arms. "Anyway, that's how I met him, and to be honest my feelings for him are starting to be scary."

"Love at first sight," Ivy said. "That's how I felt about Ray when I first met him."

"I'm not in love with the man!"

"Even if you were, you wouldn't admit it to us."

"Ivy's right," Jade agreed. "You are in love."

"I'm not in love, so let's not go there. I don't even know the man."

"But you're feeling him. I can see it in your eyes," Ivy said with a grin.

Miranda waved her hand at them and smiled. "Did anybody pray over these chips?"

CHAPTER FOUR

Sheena had thought that hanging out with her friends would make her feel better, but she went home that evening feeling more depressed than ever.

She knew the reason: Jason Tyrone Jackson. She missed him like crazy.

After showering she lay across her bed and, using the remote control, she began flipping channels. *Nothing's on I want to see*, she thought.

She turned the television off and sat at her computer to retrieve her email. She was hoping for one from Jason, but she was disappointed yet again. *I guess when he said he was finished with me he truly meant what he said.*

Their relationship had been strained since the day he walked into her office and told her how he felt about her. The message was clear; he was as straightforward as he could be. She turned off the computer and remembered how she had looked into his eyes that day.

Jason was as close to her as any of her girlfriends. He had been the only man she had felt comfortable enough with to share her intimate thoughts, her dreams and aspirations and, yes, even her desires.

Jason told her he had loved her since the first day they met. But Sheena didn't believe in love at first sight. Jason was her friend, and at times she felt as if they were brother and sister. An intimate relationship was one thing, but a sexual one was another. Jason wanted forever after and a day, wedding rings and vows.

Each time she remembered that day it brought tears to her eyes in the same way it did when she asked him…

"Why Jason, why are you doing this to us?" She did all she could to stop the tears from falling. "We agreed long ago to be the very best of friends. Why've you changed your mind now? I don't understand."

"Sheen, I can't help how I feel about you. I can't help how my body reacts to you."

She walked toward her office window, folded her arms, looking at the view outside. It was a cold and rainy day, and it mirrored her heart.

For a long time no one spoke. Then she turned to him and asked. "So what are we supposed to do? Just act as if the other doesn't exist?"

He walked over to where she stood. "I know a solution." He positioned himself directly in front of her.

"Which is?" she asked nervously.

"We can take it one step at a time. We're already the best of friends; we already do everything couples do. We just never had the romance. We can just add it as we…"

"No, Jason, I like things the way they are."

"Then I guess it's settled." He moved away from her, heading toward the door. "I asked for a transfer and it's come through. I'm leaving." There was tremendous pain in his voice, and she could feel the tears pressing against the backs of her eyes.

"It doesn't have to be this way," she choked out.

"Yes, it does. I don't want… I can't be around you."

Before she opened her mouth she knew in her heart it was the end of their friendship. "Well, you have to do what's right for you."

"And I'm sure you think you're doing what's right for you," he answered.

Sheena turned away from him, acting as if what was going on down on Market Street was of more concern to her than what was happening in her office.

He opened the door.

She looked up when she heard the office chatter penetrate from the hallway.

"Goodbye, Sheena." Without waiting for an answer from her, he closed the door gently behind him.

It was a few moments before she reacted and allowed the tears to fall, murmuring his name into the empty air, her words falling into a void.

She physically jiggled herself to ward off the memory. Just before she slipped between the sheets she prayed it would be without dreaming of Jason.

‟–‘’

Darrell came to Jade's house with a sleeping Desmond in his arms. Since it was so late, she was already in her lounging pajamas; assuming Darrell would keep the child overnight. She had been studying when she heard his car pull up. "Why did you bring him home? It's almost midnight."

"I know, but we were having so much fun, time just slipped away from me."

Jade followed Darrell into Desmond's room and drew back the spread on his bed. Darrell continued, "Then, when we finally did get on the highway to come back home, I got a flat tire. I'm surprised you weren't sleeping! What are you doing?"

"Studying, I'm trying to get a head start on the bar exam."

"Ooh, yeah?"

"Yeah." Jade went back to her bedroom, determined to get another hour of study time in. A few minutes later Darrell appeared at the door. "Well, you can let yourself out; this is still your house."

"It's your house while you're living here."

Jade simply smiled and dropped her gaze back to her book.

"Jade." Jade looked up without saying a word. "Why don't you at least consider coming to my trial sermon?"

"Because, you don't need any distractions. The tongues will be wagging as soon as I set foot in the sanctuary, and you don't need to hear gossip or to see anything negative while you're delivering your initial sermon."

"Jade, I don't care about what they say or what they think."

"Well, I do. It's not important for me to be there. Besides, Dee will be there, and so will the rest of your family."

"Just not you, right?"

"I'm not family, Darrell."

"You are to me."

She sighed. "Please, let's not do this. It's late and I really want to focus on my studies."

Darrell turned away with a sigh. Without looking at her, he said, "Why won't you even consider marrying me?"

Jade stopped looking at the text she was reading from once again. "I thought we agreed not to talk about this anymore."

Darrell turned to face her. He said, loudly, "No, I didn't agree to any such thing."

"Darrell."

Darrell moved closer to the bed, standing close to where Jade lay. "Why can't you understand that I'm in love with you?" he whispered.

"Darrell."

"What do you want from me, Jade?" Darrell sat down on the side of the bed. "What do I need to do to make you happy?" He caressed her cheek with the back of his hand. "What can I do to make us a family?"

Jade closed her eyes at the feel of his touch, knowing that she wanted more, too much more. With her eyes still closed, she asked in a whisper, "Why do you do this to me?" She opened her eyes and glared at him. "Why do you entice me?" Darrell moved his hand from her face. "Why do you tempt me this way?"

"Touching your face tempts you?"

"At this very moment I'm in agony."

Darrell stood up instantly and moved back to the door, pausing in the doorway. "Sorry, it's not my intention to tempt you or put you in a compromising position."

"You need to leave," she said flatly.

"Why won't you tell me what I need to do to get a commitment from you?"

"Being committed only means we can finish what you started here."

"That's right! I need to be morally correct, but I love you, Jade. Why can't you understand that?"

"Well, my love for you is partly the reason why I won't marry you."

"What?" Darrell dropped his arms to his side.

"Besides, you're horny, Darrell. Look at you. Every time you see me you see sex."

"That's not true!"

"Liar!" she snapped.

"I'm in love with you, Jade!"

"I'm the only woman you've ever been with, Darrell. You just *think* you're in love with me."

"No."

"Yes."

"Baby, no!"

Jade moved her books from her lap and placed them on the nightstand. "Wanna make a bet?" She stood up and walked toward him.

"What are you doing?"

"Come on, baby, let's do this," she said, her voice as sensuous as her movements.

"What?" Darrell whispered, mystified.

"Oh, yeah, let's do this. You can repent tomorrow and I promise I won't tell a soul." Jade began to unbutton her pajama top, not taking her eyes from Darrell's face. She allowed it to slide off her shoulders, down her arms, onto the floor. Darrell stared and didn't utter a word. Then she pulled the string that was tied in a bow, loosening the lounging pants, allowing them to slide down her legs. Darrell literally drooled. Jade moved even closer to him, clad in only a bra and panties. Darrell was frozen in place, afraid to move.

Jade needed to prove a point and she wanted him to get the message. So she placed her hand on his chest, and starred directly in his eyes. When his lips parted, he let out an agonized moan.

Jade smiled up at him. "You see, Darrell. It's not about love. It's about sex."

Why do I stand here and let her do this to me? He knew why. "What do you expect? I'm still a man."

"What do you expect? I'm still a heathen."

"What? Why would you say that about yourself? Do you really look at yourself that way? Because I don't see you…"

"You don't have to. I know what I am. You and I know the truth, Darrell. I'm the experienced one. I taught you everything you know, didn't I?"

Darrell's mouth dropped. Jade moved away from him and hissed, "Get out of here! Because the next time you come in here enticing me, I won't just take you to the edge, I'm going to push you off this ledge and when I'm through with you you'll have to fast for forty days and forty nights to be redeemed." Jade pushed him into the hallway and slammed the door between them.

ॐ

Darrell called Jade twice from his car as he drove home; she hung up on him both times. He was at his wits' end pondering how to make her understand that he truly loved her. After walking into his parents' home he noticed that his mother was sitting in the living room in her favorite chair, reading the Bible.

"Mom."

"Hey, baby." He paused at the front door and leaned his back against it. Under the dim lights of the entry hall his mother could see the rapid rise and fall of his shoulders and she stood up and rushed to his side. He was crying. She hadn't seen her son cry since he was a child. Something dreadful had to have happened to make him break down in tears! "What's wrong, baby?"

Darrell couldn't answer her at first. He had taken all he could take, emotionally, and he couldn't hold his feelings back any longer. The question was a simple one. "Why doesn't she want me, Mom?" He choked in despair.

Darrell's mother knew she shouldn't interfere in her grown son's life. Yet, seeing him in this state pushed her to the limit. *I'm going to talk to that Jade and find out why she's making his life a living hell.*

Sonja Parker called Jade at seven o'clock the next morning and asked her to meet her at the Highway Diner. "Without Desmond, okay, Jade?"

CHAPTER FIVE

Mrs. Parker was first to arrive at the diner.

She asked for a booth in the rear where she felt they could chat privately. When she saw Jade coming toward her fifteen minutes later, she was sorely disappointed. Jade had brought her grandson with her.

"Grandma, Grandma!" The boy rushed to his grandmother, holding his arms out for a hug.

"Hello, my sweetheart, how are you today?"

"I'm going Frank's Interlude!"

Mrs. Parker laughed. "You are?"

He nodded in excitement.

Jade sighed. "Dee, I told you it's the Franklin Institute."

"Yes, the Frank's Interlude!"

"Oh, leave him alone, Jade, he's doing just fine." His grandmother hugged him again.

"Ivy should be here any minute to get him. She's taking her kids to the Franklin Institute and she asked if she could take her godchild with her."

"Oh, how nice." She was glad to get that information. So she would be able to talk to Jade without his little ears listening, after all!

Ivy arrived, picked up Desmond, and departed again. Sonja got right to the point. "Jade, I know that I don't have a right to poke my nose in my son's personal business. I've tried to mind my own affairs, but when Darrell came home last night in a state I hadn't seen him in since he was a boy, I was provoked to ask you to meet with me."

Jade sat her fork down, moved her plate to the side and rested her hands on the table, folding them in front of her. "I see." Jade knew Darrell had been upset when he'd left the night before. But she never expected he was so upset that it would cause his mother alarm.

"My son is hurting and you are causing his pain. And I'd really like to know why. I mean, I know what he feels for you and it hurts me to see him so unhappy. You're killing him, Jade. He doesn't have the same zeal he had. What did he do to you to deserve such pain?"

"It's not my desire to hurt your son, Mrs. Parker. We didn't even argue last night. I simply proved a point while teaching him a lesson."

"A lesson."

"Yes, a lesson." Jade lowered her gaze, wondering how much to tell Darrell's mother. "Your son likes to push me to the edge. Well, last night, I pushed back."

"What lesson?"

"That it's not about love, it's about hormones. I believe you understand what I mean."

Sonja Parker wiped her hands with her napkin and dropped it in her plate. "I've been living for some years now and I'm not as dumb to the world as you may think. I ain't been saved all my life, young lady."

"Mrs. Parker, I'm not…"

The older woman held up her hand to stop Jade from talking. "And I've never seen a man cry because of his hormones. What I witnessed last night came from that boy's heart. Only love can make a man weep uncontrollably."

"He's your son, Mrs. Parker. And I'm sure if I saw Dee under the same circumstances I would be doing the same thing you are now. But the fact of the matter is, I've been honest with Darrell. I told him we would never be together again. It's him that pushes this issue, not me."

"The other day you told me you loved him."

"I do love him. I love him so much that I'm willing to give up my only son to him."

"What?"

"After last night, I prayed and thought some things through. The best thing for me to do is to move out of his house…"

"Jade, what are you talkin' about?"

"I'm going to give him Dee."

"What? Why would you do that when the thing that bothered you most was losing your son?"

"I won't be losing him. I'll be giving him to his father. Besides, Darrell can teach him to be a man after God's own heart. And I'm willing to sacrifice my…" Jade was so choked up with emotion that she couldn't complete the sentence at first. "I'm willing to give up my only son and sacrifice my own happiness for them. You talking to me today only give me confirmation that that's exactly what I should do."

"Jade, now let's not react in haste. I know I shouldn't have interfered in my son's life but…"

"Mrs. Parker, I've thought about what you said. You know about me being selfish. And you're right. I am selfish. But giving Desmond to Darrell will be the most unselfish thing that I'll ever do." Jade stood up. "I really need to go while I have some control over myself. Please excuse me. You have a nice day, Mrs. Parker." Jade didn't wait for an answer.

Sonja Parker watched as Jade weaved her way out of the diner.

๛

Jade was angry enough to spit bullets when she left the restaurant.

After driving out of the parking lot she pulled into the K-Mart lot to get her temper under control. *Why did I tell her I was giving my son to Darrell?* She asked herself. No way was she going to give her son away! Jade make a fist and banged it against the steering wheel several times. *You're stronger than this,* she told herself. *Don't let this woman get to you.*

Jade's cell phone rang. She took a deep breath as she stared at it. She needed to calm down before answering it. *You've been through worse, so get it together, girl.* She looked at the display: it was Darrell's cell phone number. She really didn't want to talk to him, so she let it ring, allowing her voice mail to get it.

After some time passed, Jade had calmed down. She searched in her purse for her wallet, making sure she found her ATM card. She put the car in drive and headed toward highway 42 going to the Atlantic City expressway.

It took forty-five minutes for Jade to drive to the Trump Plaza. She had no idea she would be coming to the casino. But she needed to get away and relax her mind from all the drama surrounding her. Keith certainly had started making her nervous.

As she pulled in the valet parking section of the hotel, she noticed Greg Farmer leaning against a post. Greg and Jade had met when she returned to Rutgers to finish law school. Greg was barely passing until he and Jade became study partners.

Greg's jacket was pulled up tightly on his neck and he had on a gray wool cap. Needless to say, it was cold and windy.

Greg squinted his eyes when he saw Jade's car then widened with surprise once he recognized her; and immediately he came over to her car.

"Well, Sanders, I'm surprised to find you here."

"All I can say is that this is a small world." She allowed him to kiss her cheek. "I thought you stopped smoking."

"I did, then I got Professor Jacobs, and I started back again." Jade laughed loudly. "That's not funny, Sanders."

"You avoided him last semester just to put it off until this semester!" She continued to laugh.

"Yeah, well, I guess I see the humor. You drove here by yourself?"

"Sure did. Are you here alone?"

"No, my brother and a few of his friends came down about two hours ago. I lost about a hundred bucks. I can't handle it. I have to buy gas and eat until my next paycheck."

"Well, maybe you can give me some luck. If you aren't leaving, come in with me while I wrestle the one-armed bandit."

"You and me?"

Jade smiled, "Yeah, Greg, you and me."

"I like the sound of that."

Greg and Jade played the slot machines for hours. For the time being, Jade forgot about her problems and enjoyed playing the games. When the night was over, Jade had won over a thousand dollars and Greg won back the money he'd lost – along with a few hundred dollars in winnings.

Greg found his brother sitting at the blackjack table and learned that he wouldn't be going home until the next day. So Greg asked Jade if he could get a ride back with her.

"I'm really enjoying hanging out with you, Sanders," Greg said as he watched Jade go to the passenger side of her car when the attendant pulled the car up.

"Good, then you won't mine driving us back." She grinned at him.

"Oh, is that the only way I can get a ride home?"

"Not unless you want to risk your life. 'Cause I'm tired."

"Well, in all honesty, Sanders. I'm thankful for the ride. This way I can get home and get some study time in."

"I need to do the same."

"Why don't we study together? You can come over to my place and…"

"No way! That's out of the question."

"Sanders, I promise to be a complete gentlemen. I've had the hots for you, I'll admit it, but I'm the kind of man that respects a lady."

Jade smiled. "I know you are, Greg. It's just that I like you and I don't want us to get into any compromising positions."

"I understand your concern, but there's no need for it. I would never do that."

"You may not intentionally do it. But it's happened to me on more than one occasion." Greg handed the attendant two dollars and got into the car. Jade buckled up her seat belt.

He did the same. "Did I ever tell you I was married before?"

"No, I didn't know that."

"Well, I was," he said, easing out into the street. "She divorced me and married her dentist. I couldn't provide for her as she felt I should so she found herself someone who could." Greg looked over at Jade as he stopped at a red light. "I thought I was in love with her. When she left me I didn't think I would be able to survive it." He shrugged. "I registered for classes and finished up my degree in business. It took me a year and half to get my degree. Then I came straight to law school. One year after law school I met you." He paused as he merged the car onto the Atlantic City expressway. Jade remained silent. "You were a breath of fresh air. I didn't think women like you truly existed." He placed his hand on Jade's and patted it.

"You're making me blush."

"Well, I'm only telling you the truth. I've never met a more sincere woman than you in my life. You're honest and straightforward, and I really don't know if you're going to make it as an attorney-at-law." Both of them laughed. "But I do know I admire you."

"I admire you too, Greg. Remember when we first met you had all intentions of dropping out and finding you a job with bankers hours?"

"How can I forget?"

"Well, you buckled down, worked hard and studied long hours and look at you now. You've turned a 2.2 grade point average to a 3.5 in a year and a half, that's impressive."

"You're a good teacher, Jade. I'm lucky I met you."

"I don't believe in luck."

"Well, I'm blessed that I met you." They smiled at each other. "Toll."

"I have it."

"No, this is on me. You may not believe in luck, but I do. I'm going home with over three hundred dollars in winnings because of you. So I have the tolls."

Jade's cell phone rang. She looked at the caller ID. "Darrell," she said to Greg.

Greg nodded. "Answer it. You've been avoiding him all day."

"No, I haven't."

"Answer it, Sanders."

She sighed and pushed the button. "Hello?"

"Where are you, Jade?" Greg could hear Darrell's voice, it was so loud.

"I'm on my way home."

"I've been calling you all day."

"What do you want, Darrell? You don't have Dee, so it can't be about him."

"We need to talk."

"About what?"

"About what you and my mother argued about this morning.'

"I didn't argue with your mother."

"She said you were talking some nonsense about giving Dee to me."

"She's right, that was nonsense."

Greg touched Jade's arm and pointed to the gas gage. "You need gas," he whispered.

"Okay, let's stop at the next station."

"Who's with you?"

"I'll be home in about an hour or so. Okay?"

Darrell raised his voice louder, "I want to know who you're with."

Jade knew Greg could hear Darrell. When she looked over at him he murmured, "Tell him."

Jade closed her eyes tightly. "I'm with Greg."

"Greg? You mean Greg from school?"

"Yes, that Greg. Look I'll be home in about an hour. 'Bye." Jade hung up the phone.

Greg kept his eyes on the road. "He's pretty demanding for you and him not to have a more personal relationship?"

Jade didn't answer Greg. But he was right and it was something she was going to have to put a stop to.

CHAPTER SIX

Sheena sat next to Josephine, her new bowling partner, as she packed up her gear. They had practiced for two hours to get ready for a tournament that Sheena had signed herself and Jason up for – over six months ago. This was their first practice together, and Sheena could tell that she had a much better chance of winning this year's tournament with her new partner than she would have had with Jason. Josephine was an excellent player.

Sheena turned her head in the direction of the clapping. "Sheena, Sheena, Sheena, you're rolling over those pins like you're after my trophy and prize money!"

A wide smile lit up Sheena's face as she saw who was speaking. Jose was the son of Pastor Tito Santos. Pastor Santos had the largest congregation of Hispanics in Camden. He'd started his ministry after leaving the Catholic Church and was now a part of the Church of God and Christ. The church's membership had grown from twelve to twelve hundred in less than three years.

It was Jose and his outreach ministry that evangelized people from the streets to the church.

"Hey, Jose!" Sheena stood and gave him a big hug. "How you been – and where is Penny?"

"Penny's at home. She's pregnant and wasn't up to hanging out with me today."

"She's pregnant again?"

Jose nodded. "And, if this one isn't a girl, we'll try again. I haven't seen you at the lanes in a while. I thought maybe you gave up since you lost your bowling partner."

"Well, I'm back and I have a new one now. Come here, let me introduce you! Josephine Knight, this is Jose Santos. He belongs to the *other league*," Sheena said with emphasis.

"Very nice to meet you, lovely lady." Jose took her hand and, as was his custom, he lifted her hand to his lips and kissed it.

Josephine was put off by the gesture and quickly pulled her hand away. "Hello," she answered, eying him with some scrutiny.

"You know you could've moved over to the winning league after Jason left. Why you'd want to stay with the losers is beyond me."

"I stick with my league through good times and bad times," Sheena said stoutly.

"The problem is your league never has good times!" He bellowed with laughter.

"Have your laugh now, 'cause you may not be laughing long," she retorted, though she was laughing too. "My new partner is rough."

"Yeah, I noticed she has skills. I was watching you two."

"I'm going to get some lemonade," Josephine interrupted. She turned to Sheena. "Want some?"

"No, thanks."

"Be right back."

Jose watched as Josephine walked away. "She's not too friendly, is she?"

"She's not real talkative with people she doesn't know, that's all. But she's a nice lady."

Jose leaned on the back of the chair next to Sheena. "How long've you known her?"

"I work with her. She's one of our department's investigators."

"So, you really don't know her that well."

"Not really," Sheena conceded. "This is our first practice. Hopefully, she'll help me win your trophy!"

Jose laughed. "What church does she belong to?"

"I don't know. Come to think of it, I've never asked."

He nodded. "Uh, I noticed that she has on a rainbow bracelet – and so do you."

"Oh, this?"

Jose nodded.

Sheena stuck out her arm. "Yeah, I think it's adorable. She had hers first and I told her I really liked the colors on it. Yesterday she came into my office and gave it to me. It was really sweet of her, wasn't it?"

It was clear to Jose that Sheena had no idea what the bracelet signified. He thought for a moment about how to tell her what it meant.

Sheena was still talking. "Josephine says she's had good luck since she started wearing hers. Of course, as you well know, I don't believe in luck." Sheena touched the gold cross hanging on a chain around her neck. "I believe in being blessed: that's why I wear a cross."

"I agree with you. That's why I couldn't understand why you're wearing a symbol that signifies gay pride."

"What? This bracelet?"

He nodded. "That's what it means."

Sheena stared at the man as if he had two heads. "I liked all the colors on it and I just thought that it was cute."

Jose shrugged. "Well, if you're not gay and you don't want people to think that you are, you need to lose the bracelet."

Sheena removed the bracelet from her arm and pushed it into the pocket of her jeans.

Jose wasn't finished, however. "It seems to me that you and your new friend are unequally yoked. You know what the Word says about hanging around unbelievers. She'll end up drawing you into her way of life, so watch yourself."

"She could be like me, Jose. Maybe she doesn't know the bracelet is worn to show your sexual orientation."

"Maybe, maybe not. Hold on for a minute, let me give you something." Jose went to where he'd been sitting and grabbed a briefcase. When he reached Sheena he opened it. Inside were all kinds of gospel leaflets. He pulled out one called *The Big Lie*. He handed it to Sheena. "You know me," he said, smiling. "I'm always armed to steer someone to the truth so they can be set free."

Sheena smiled.

"This pamphlet is about homosexuality. It's based on scripture. Read it, okay?"

"I will."

"I'm out of here. Tell Jason to give me a call?"

"Sure, Jose. Tell Penny I said hello. And don't you forget to invite me to the baby shower I'm sure someone will be giving her." She hugged him. "And thank you for the heads-up."

"You're welcome, Ms. Sheena. Be safe."

She nodded and waved goodbye.

While Sheena waited for Josephine, she began to read the leaflet and she was so engrossed in it that she didn't know her friend had returned.

"You ready to go?" Josephine asked.

"Um, yeah… I'm ready."

๙ඏ

Sheena couldn't get what Jose told her about the bracelet out of her head. She studied Josephine as they sat at Friendly Restaurant looking for signs of homosexuality. Nothing. Maybe Josephine was just as ignorant about the meaning of the bracelet as she was. Sheena wanted to ask her, but decided against it. How do you just come out and ask a person if they are gay? *No,* she thought, *I can't ask her that. I hardly know the woman.*

"I think I'm going to get a banana split," Josephine announced as she perused the menu.

"I dare don't try anything that sweet. How do you eat that stuff and not gain a pound?"

"I think I have an extra-active metabolism."

"Must be nice to be blessed that way."

Josephine abruptly slammed her menu down in front of her, startling Sheena. She looked over at the man sitting at the table across from them and said, "Do you mind? You've been staring over here since we sat down at this table!"

"Josephine…" Sheena said warningly.

Josephine rolled her eyes at the man as she slowly turned her head and looked at Sheena. "Don't that bother you?"

"Josephine, that was totally unnecessary." Sheena looked around. "Why would you want to cause a scene?"

The waiter had arrived. "Are you ready to place your order?"

"Yes," Josephine answered. "I want a banana split with extra cherries."

"And for you?" he asked Sheena.

"Pepsi, please."

"Okay, be right back with your orders."

Sheena looked over at the young man to whom Josephine had spoken so harshly. He never did look her way. "Why'd you do that, Josephine? The guy wasn't doing us any harm."

"The guy's been staring over here since we sat down."

"Lower your voice, you're embarrassing me!"

Josephine looked surprised. "Oh, excuse me! I thought you hate it when men look at you that way."

"There's different kinds of looks. That guy had a look of admiration. He wasn't lusting. I know the look of lust when I see it. Besides, he was only looking."

Josephine looked over at the guy who was now looking down at his plate. "They're all dogs, Sheena."

"I disagree."

"Oh, you do? Then, why aren't you with Jason?"

She shrugged. "Jason wanted more and I liked our relationship as it was."

"No, Jason's a dog like all the rest of them and he wanted to jump your bones." Josephine looked to Sheena for a comeback, and when none came, she said, "You can't even befriend them, Sheena. They're always after self-gratification."

"Jason's not like that."

"Really, let me count. How many women has Jason dated since I've been working in the Philadelphia office? Six, ten, twenty?"

"Wow, you've been trying to keep count?"

"No."

"You have a crush on him?"

"Hell, no!"

Sheena sighed. "I've been thinking about Jason a lot since he left, and personally, I think he's handsome, he has a good head on his shoulders, he's employed, and he's fun to be with."

"So, tell me again, Sheena, why aren't you with him?"

"Josephine?" A man came up to them. "I thought it was you! It's been a long time. How you been?"

"Fine, Perry. How 'bout you?"

"Great! Let me introduce you to my wife. Tina, this is Josephine." The woman beside him extended her hand. "You mean the Josephine you grew up with?"

"The one and only."

"Well, it's a pleasure meeting you. Now I can put a face to all the stories."

Josephine shook her hand. "I hope he's not bad-mouthing me!"

"Everything I told her is the truth, including you breaking my heart." Perry looked at Josephine who made no comment. "And who is your friend?" Perry finally took a look at Sheena and, as most men did, stared at her with his mouth open.

"Perry, this is Sheena Daniels; Sheena, Perry and his wife – I'm sorry, your name again?"

"Tina."

"Nice meeting both of you." Sheena touched Tina's extended belly. "So, when is the baby due?"

"Excuse me, your orders," the waiter announced.

Perry smiled. "I see you still like splits with extra cherries."

"Yeah." Josephine grinned at him. "Some old habits are hard to break."

Tina was staring at Sheena. "So, when's the baby due?" she asked again.

"Any day now." Tina looked away.

"Your first?" Josephine asked.

"It is."

"Well, I know the two of you are excited," Sheena said with a smile.

"We're ecstatic." Perry answered.

"I'm going to sit down, honey. My back is killing me. Again, nice meeting you ladies."

Perry pointed at Josephine's banana split. "Enjoy." He followed his wife.

Josephine started eating.

Sheena leaned forward. "Okay, here's the deal. I'll tell you why I'm not with Jason if you tell me why you broke that man's heart."

Josephine's spoon stopped in mid-air. "Perry is old news, real old news." She pushed the spoon in her mouth.

"That may be so, but he seems like a nice man."

"He is."

"Oh, *he*'s not a dog?"

"All men are dogs. Didn't you see how he stared at you?

Sheena took a sip of Pepsi. "His wife stared too, does that make her a dog?"

Josephine put her spoon down. She looked at Sheena for a moment. "It was wrong of me to compare you to the average woman. I guess in your case men and women do stare at you." Josephine picked up her spoon. "Your beauty attracts people in general."

Sheena looked at the rainbow bracelet Josephine wore on her wrist. Though Sheena was an attorney, she never did any litigating. In her line of work she acted as a judge and interpreted the law for the U.S. Department of Education. She wondered, *how could I lead up to asking this woman if she's gay?*

"I guess you're not gonna tell me why Jason asked to be transferred to the Atlanta office."

"You'll have to ask him that question."

"I don't think I have to ask. He finally saw the light. They always find out about us. Even if we deny it, what's in us comes out."

"What do you mean?" Sheena stared at her.

"You've told me you aren't as comfortable around men as you are with women."

"So…" Sheena protested.

"Have you ever asked yourself why?"

Sheena ignored her. "Tell me about the bracelet you're wearing on your wrist."

"I see you took yours off," Josephine said softly. "I know what I am, Sheena. I've accepted it and I don't mind identifying myself by wearing this bracelet."

Sheena kept a blank face. *So, she is gay.*

"Did you just come out and tell Perry?"

"No, Perry caught me in bed with his cousin – who he knew was a lesbian."

"So your boyfriend's cousin was the one who turned you out?"

"No, actually, I've known since I was a child. I just fought it for years because I wanted to be what was considered normal." Josephine looked over to where Perry was sitting. "If I'd had my choice, I'd be sitting over there with Perry with my belly full. But I have no choice in the matter. I was born this way."

"Well, you need to get born again." Sheena reached into her jeans pocket and pulled out the rainbow bracelet and pushed it in front of Josephine. "I didn't know what this was when I put it on. Jose told me what it means, so I took it off."

"I figured as much."

Sheena sipped her soda. "Well, you also need to know that I'm a Christian. And even if I felt like I was gay, I'd never act on it.

"So you'd rather live miserable than to be happy?"

"This life is short. Death is eternal. It's my choice to spend eternity in heaven and not in hell. I'd rather do God's will and obey His commandments while I'm here on earth so that I can be assured that once I close my eyes and am resting in my grave, I'll be with Jehovah, living happily ever after."

Josephine paused with her spoon halfway to her mouth. "So you think I'm going to hell?"

"No, I don't *think* any such thing. I know you're going to hell if you continue on the road you're on."

"I see theologians have brainwashed you."

Sheena thought about the comment for a moment. "Yes, it's true. I've been persuaded to believe that everything in the Bible is the truth. I was taught not to deviate from it. And you know what, I'm glad I was taught from my mother's womb. Nevertheless, it was my choice. God doesn't force anyone to believe in Him. I choose to be a believer."

"You were programmed to be a believer. You just said it yourself, from your mother's womb."

"And somehow, somewhere, somebody programmed you to think you're gay."

"I was born this way."

"You had a choice, Josephine. You still do. The choice has always been up to you. It's called free will. God gave us free will to pick and choose. To make our own decisions."

Josephine shook her head. "God made me. And I don't think that He's as narrow-minded as people are. He loves me, just like He loves you."

"Yes, He does love you. But He hates sin. Anything that's against His word is sin." Sheena pulled out the pamphlet Jose had given her. She pushed it across the table to Josephine. "Look, I'd like you to read this. It's gives scripture references on this subject."

Josephine made no move to take the booklet.

Sheena persevered. "Look, let me read a few of the scriptures for you." She pointed to a section. "In Leviticus 18:22, the scripture says, Thou shalt not lie with mankind, as with womankind: it is *abomination*. And in Leviticus 20:13, If a man also lie with mankind, as he lieth with a woman, both of them have committed an *abomination*: The key word here is abomination. It means God hates it. It's disgraceful and unholy to Him."

Josephine just stared at Sheena.

"Look, I know this little pamphlet isn't going to make you change your mind right now. But I hope it will get you to search for the truth. So please just read it." Sheena pushed it in front of her. "And another thing, you and I can't be bowling partners, after all."

"What?"

"I'll find another partner." Sheena's cell phone rang. "Hello"

"Hey, Sheen."

"Jade! What's up?"

"I just drove up to Greg's apartment complex and guess who I just bumped into arguing with his girlfriend."

Sheena looked over at Josephine. "Pardon me," she said to the other woman, who still had a stunned look on her face. "I'm clueless. Who did you see?"

"Pastor Owens."

"What! Did he see you?"

"You know he did. Girl, the man's eyes almost bulged from his head."

"Oh, I wish I could have been a fly on the wall! Hold on a minute." Sheena directed her attention back to Josephine as she stood. "Look, I have to go." She turned to walk away.

"I don't understand why we can't compete together in the tournament!" Josephine protested.

Sheena stopped and answered, "I'd tell you. But you wouldn't understand it."

When Sheena got outside the restaurant she remembered Jade was on the phone. "You still there?"

"I was about to hang up. Where are you?"

"I had stopped to get a burger with Josephine."

"She's your new bowling partner, right."

"Wrong, she's history."

"I thought you said she had skills."

"She's gay."

"What? Did she try to..."

Sheena snorted. "Please, I'm not talking to you from jail, am I?"

"Did she just come out and tell you?"

Sheena told Jade what happened as she got into her car and drove home. "When I walked out the restaurant I told the woman she'd never understand it."

"No, you're right. She wouldn't understand that it's commanded of us to be separated from unbelievers."

"She'd never understand because darkness can't comprehend the light. Enough about her. Tell me about Owens, girl!"

Jade paused. "Look, I just got home myself. I'm pulling up into the driveway now. Let me get in the house and I'll call you back."

"You better call me right back, too!"

Jade saw Darrell spying on her from the living room window. She knew an argument was brewing. "On second thought, let me tell you now." Jade got out of the car. Darrell opened the front door before she reached it and held it open for her. "Hold on a minute, Sheen." Jade walked in past Darrell, removed her coat and hung it in the hall closet.

"I want to talk to you in the living room," Darrell barked.

Jade turned slowly in his direction. "Do you mind? I'm on the phone!" Jade held out her cell phone.

Darrell's nose began to flare. He paused before answering. "Then when you're done." He turned and walked into the living room.

Jade blew out a sigh. She knew there was no way to avoid what was ahead. She put the phone back to her ear. "I'm back."

"Hey, we can talk later. It sounds like Darrell's pissed with you."

"He can wait."

"He called me today, looking for you."

"I went to AC."

"You were in Atlantic City?"

"Yes. Now do you want to hear about Owens or what?" Jade passed the living room where Darrell was waiting and went into the family room.

"Oh, do tell!"

"I met Greg in AC. We hung out for a few hours playing the slots. Then he asked if I could give him a ride home. He lives in Mt. Laurel. Anyway, when we got to his apartment complex I saw this woman arguing with someone in a black BMW. And she was loud! She kept saying, *I hate you, Preston.* I couldn't understand what the other person in the car was saying. Then Greg said, *not again.*"

"Who was it?" asked Sheena.

"That's what I asked Greg. And he said it was his cousin and her boyfriend. Then he said, you know, I don't understand women sometimes. My cousin says she doesn't want to be with him, but she can't help herself. But there's no future for her with the man, 'cause he's married."

"That *is* a problem," conceded Sheena. "So, what happened next?"

"Well, Greg said that he wouldn't leave his cousin alone. And while we're sitting there, she took something from the car and headed for the building, and the man goes in right after her."

"Ooh, no! Don't tell me it was Owens!"

"I swear, Sheena, I couldn't believe my eyes. But it was Pastor Owens!"

Jade remembered how she'd felt when she first saw him. She blinked. Hard. *Maybe my eyes are playing tricks on me,* she thought. "Oh, my God!" Her mouth was agape. She took a deep breath and continued talking to Sheena. "I told Greg he was the one who talked me into doing all that extra tutoring, and that he was the pastor at Greater Mount Hope."

"And what did Greg say?"

"He said that's why he stopped going to church, 'cause ministers like him cripple the whole Christian community."

"Ooh, girl, I can't believe this. Then what happened?" Sheena was fascinated.

Jade sighed. "Then Greg invited *me* in. He said he wanted to see the look on Pastor Owens' face when he saw me."

"No!"

"Yes, he pulled the keys out of the ignition so I couldn't drive away," Jade said. "But then who comes out of the building but his cousin, Cheri, and she's all upset, and Pastor Owens is right there behind her. You should have seen his expression when he saw me, girl! Miranda was right, after all: the man's nothing but a hypocrite."

"So then what happened?" Sheena demanded.

"Owens got in his car. All the while Greg's there talkin' to his cousin, and she's clearly upset. I'm in the middle saying, give me my keys so I can go home."

"Owens didn't say a word to you?" Sheena asked.

"Not a word."

"That man is going to bust hell wide open. You better get away from him and his crooked ministry, girl. You know when you wallow with dogs, you get up with fleas."

"Owens and I are not friends, believe me. He pays me to tutor and that's it. Besides, why should the kids suffer because of him?"

"God don't bless mess, Jade."

"That may be so, but he can bless *through* anyone, even someone as crooked as Pastor Owens."

Sheena laughed. "Yeah, I guess you're right. And you've had time to think about it."

Jade spied Darrell staring at her. "Look, I have to go. Call me tomorrow, all right?"

"Will do. 'Bye."

Jade could tell Darrell wasn't happy. She knew he was going to drill her about her whereabouts so she prepared herself for the interrogation.

"Where have you been?" he barked.

"Out," Jade said without explaining. She walked down the hall toward her bedroom. Darrell caught up with her.

"I'm talking to you."

"I hear you, and so do the neighbors."

"Then answer me."

"I did answer you. I said I was out."

"I know you were out, Jade. Where have you been? I called Ivy and she hadn't heard from you since she saw you with my mother. I called your mother and she hadn't heard from you at all. I called Sheena and she was bowling with her new partner and nobody heard from you."

"Well, I talked to *you*."

"That was an hour ago. I was worried."

"Well, I'm sorry that you were worried. But I'm fine and I'm tired. I want to shower and go to bed. So if you'll excuse me, you can let yourself out." Jade closed her bedroom door, leaving Darrell alone in the hallway.

Jade went into the bathroom. Twenty minutes later she was feeling refreshed. After massaging her face with moisturizer, she slipped into her satin robe and secured it tightly around her waist. She looked out the window. "What the…" she whispered, and then blew out a sigh. Darrell's car was still there.

When she opened the bedroom door Darrell was there, in the hallway, leaning against the wall.

"I thought you were gone." She brushed past him, heading for the kitchen.

He followed her.

She opened the refrigerator, pulled out the apple juice and poured herself a glass. "Want some?" She glared at him.

"Who's Keith Strickland?"

Jade almost dropped the glass she was offering him. She walked over to the sink in an effort to get her emotions under control. "Did he call?"

"Yeah, while you were in the shower. So who is he?"

Jade felt that she could have fallen through the floor. She collected herself quickly. "He's from North

Carolina." She didn't want to lie, so she answered truthfully. "We hadn't seen each other since we were kids. He… uh… well, he got in touch with me… a few weeks ago."

"He told me that. So what's going on between you and Greg?"

Jade was glad he was done with wanting to know about Keith. "What do you mean, what's going on? We're friends." She took a sip of her juice and started out of the kitchen.

Darrell grabbed her by the arm, "Don't walk away from me, I'm talking to you."

"You want to argue, and I don't feel like arguing with you tonight." Darrell wasn't just angry with her, he was hostile; and Jade hadn't expected it.

"I don't care what you feel like doing. We're going to get some things straight right now. And the first thing is, I don't want you seeing Greg anymore."

"Excuse me?" She was baffled. *Did I hear that right?*

As if reading her thoughts, he said, "You heard me. No more Greg."

"Is that why I'm here in your house? So you can control who I can see?"

He took a deep breath. "I'm not trying to control you. I care about you, Jade! I need to know that you're safe."

She was angry, too. "I lived in Maryland without you. Once I graduate, I'll be living without you again. I'm a big girl, Darrell. I can handle myself."

"Is Greg helping you to handle yourself?"

She pulled away from him and went to the front door, Darrell followed behind her. Jade opened the door wide and stood back. "It's time for you to go." Her voice was cold. He didn't move, and her temper flared. "Have you lost your mind, Darrell? Get out, now."

"Damned right I've lost my mind! It's you that's making me crazy!"

Jade stopped, hearing the plea in his voice. He looked at her. "You said there was nothing going on between the two of you."

"Oh, is that what this is about? Is that why you're here? You think I'm sleeping with him?"

Why am I here? Darrell wondered. He could only stare at her. He was frustrated with not being able to have her, and afraid someone else would. He didn't know what to do to convince her that he loved and adored her.

Jade stared at him. "You're jealous! That's what this is about. Why are you jealous?"

Big boys don't cry. Grown men don't cry, he told himself. "I can't help myself, Jade." He didn't even try to deny it. He felt like crumbling to the floor. "I don't know what to do. I've tried not to feel the way I do about you." His eyes were filling with tears.

"What did I do to make you not love me?" The pain was unmistakable.

"It's not about me not loving you."

"I can't leave the ministry, Jade." He sounded desperate.

She gestured helplessly. "And I don't want you to."

"But ever since I got this call, you've pushed me away."

"It's not that, Darrell, and it's not you: it's me. I've told you I can't go on that mission with you."

"But why? You won't tell me why." He could barely speak for the pain.

"God didn't call me to the ministry."

"You act like you're an atheist."

"I didn't grow up like you. I don't have the same values you have."

"Does Greg have the same values you have?"

Her impatience with him simmered again. *Is that all that men think about?* "Greg and I are friends, that's all!"

"Why are you seeing him outside of school?"

She knew she didn't have to explain. "Look, I was upset with your mother. I just started driving. I ended up in Atlantic City. I just happened to see Greg there, that's all."

She paused and watched him as he leaned against the wall. Darrell, who was six feet even and outweighed Jade by more than fifty pounds, seemed at that moment like a small child.

Jade took a deep breath, making a decision. "Darrell." She whispered his name. When he looked down at her he saw what he hadn't seen in years. Love. He opened his arms and she went to him without a word.

Jade closed her eyes and buried her face against his chest. He felt good, too good. But at the moment she didn't care.

After a while, she tried to pull away, but Darrell wouldn't let her go. When she tilted her head to look up at him he pressed his lips against hers.

The kiss was adoring, not lustful. Jade immersed herself in the feel of its pleasure. Darrell deepened the kiss and then raised his head, still not letting her go.

"This is dangerous, Darrell," she whispered.

"Marry me, Jade. I'm not gonna stop asking you. You'll have to give in sooner or later."

"I can't," she said, tears in her eyes now, too.

"Yes, you can. You love me, girl, and I love you." Darrell lifted his right hand and traced the edge of her face with his fingertip.

Jade was weak. She shut her eyes tightly and thought, *maybe if I just rushed the words from my lips, telling him who Keith Strickland really is. How I carried his child and gave it up for adoption. Then maybe, just maybe, he would understand. Being a minister's wife is just not in my makeup.* But if she did that, she would have to come totally clean with everything – and she wasn't ready to do that. Not now, maybe not ever.

"Marry me," he repeated breathlessly.

Jade stood on tiptoe to kiss him briefly. "If I didn't want the best for you, I would."

"Why do you think you're not best for me?"

"'Cause I know me."

"I know you, too. Probably better than you know yourself. Now make me understand why you think you're not good for me." He tilted his head down to look into her eyes.

Again Jade tried to pull away. "Let me go."

"I will if you tell me what I want to know."

"You want me to tell you just how awful I really am?"

His voice turned serious. "Did you kill somebody?"

"No!"

"Well, it doesn't matter, 'cause even if you had, there's forgiveness for you." Jade remained silent and Darrell pressed on. "I was talking to Pastor Owens today."

Jade was surprised. "You had a conversation with Owens?"

Darrell laughed out loud. "I know you're surprised, but we talked a long time, and I can honestly say I feel some sympathy for the man."

"I saw him tonight."

"Who, Owens?"

"Yes."

"Where?"

"In front of Greg's apartment complex. He was arguing with a woman. Greg told me the woman was his cousin and Owens was her boyfriend."

Darrell took Jade by the hand, leading her to the living room. "Let's sit down. I don't want you to get upset with me. But I told Owens a little more about us than I should have."

"But you never liked Owens!"

"Well, I really needed to talk to someone. You had me in knots today, and he was there. Besides, it's not *Owens* I don't like. It's the controversy that surrounds him. I don't like how he treats his wife… publicly. The man is a known adulterer," Darrell pointed out.

Jade nodded. "Yes, I now know that to be a fact."

"Well… when we talked today, he revealed a lot about himself. But I don't want to talk about Owens. I want to talk about us. I want you to say you'll marry me."

Jade looked into Darrell's eyes and shook her head.

Darrell's face darkened with disappointment. "Just think about it, seriously think about it," he insisted.

"I *have* seriously thought about it." Her voice was filled with despair.

"Then pray. 'Cause if you don't marry me there's a chance I'll end up in a loveless marriage with a woman I care nothing for. Is that what you want for me? Do you want me to be unhappy?

"No …" Her voice trailed off uncertainly.

Darrell got on one knee in front of her. "Then marry me."

She stared at him. Praying, silently, *"Help me, Lord,"* she dropped her head.

"Fast and pray, Jade, God will give you the answer."

She nodded. He stood up. "I better leave before I'm tempted to do something immoral."

Jade stood and went to the door, opening it for him. "Goodnight, Darrell."

He placed a kiss on her forehead. "Good night, sweetheart."

After shutting the door behind him, Jade went directly to her room. She knelt by her bed and prayed, "God, it's me again. I don't know what to do. So I'm giving it all to you. Thy will be done. Only you know my dilemma. Only you know my fears. My heart is heavy and I'm confused. I only want to do what's right." She took a deep breath. "Why has my life become more complicated? What am I doing wrong? Even when the temptation is great I never, ever yield. I've denied my body's desires. What more should I do? What more..." Jade had never been a crybaby, but lately crying was all she had done. She let the tears flow.

"I read in your Word that your yoke is easy... and your burdens are light. If that's so, why does it feel like I'm carrying the load alone? Help... me, Lord. I can't do this alone. Why won't he let go? What do I need to do? Talk to me... Speak to me... Help me... Show me what to do." She lowered her body until her forehead touched the floor. "Please Lord, I need you, I need you."

CHAPTER SEVEN

Jade had expected Keith to contact her on Sunday, but she didn't hear a word from him.

However, Pastor Owens did. He turned up, unexpected and uninvited, at her house. "Good evening, Jade."

"Pastor Owens," Jade said, feeling stunned.

"You weren't in church today. Did you attend somewhere else?"

"No, I didn't go anywhere today."

Pastor Owens nodded but didn't pursue the thought. "I saw Darrell at the general assembly yesterday. We talked for quite a while."

"I know, he told me."

He cleared his throat. "I'd like to speak with you if I can."

"You're speaking to me now."

He smiled engagingly. "Can I come in?"

Jade folded her arms across her chest. "You should have called and asked me. You know the number … Pastor."

"You're right. Forgive me. But after that little incident yesterday, I figured you'd turn me down."

"And you'd be right."

He sighed. "I know you don't trust me. I know you may even have lost respect for me. But if you would allow me to talk with you, I promise I won't take up too much of your time. I'm sure we can, at the very least, agree to disagree."

"I'm really not in the mood for talking." Jade was wishing he would get to the point.

He looked straight at her. "Darrell cancelled his trial sermon … indefinitely."

She didn't say anything.

"Naturally, I asked him why. He told me he needed to concentrate on his relationship with you."

She felt a flutter in her chest. "He didn't tell me he cancelled," she said softly.

Pressing his advantage, he asked her again, "May I come in?"

Jade stepped back. "I'm surprised that Darrell would talk to you about personal matters."

"Well, he's a man at his wits' end, so to speak." She stood back from the door, a little ungraciously. "Oh, thank you."

She gestured him inside. "We can sit here in the family room. Uh … can I get you … anything? Something to drink?"

"No, no; thank you."

"Have a seat." Jade waited until he sat, then chose the chair opposite him.

Pastor Owens picked up the book Jade had been reading just before he rang the doorbell and read aloud. "*Victory Day By Day,* by the Reverend Dr. Arlene Churn."

"I just started reading it. I read another book she wrote, back when my father died, *The End Is Just The Beginning*."

"Oh, yes. I have that one."

"The book really helped me get through the grieving period."

"I know her. She's a gifted author and an even more gifted minister."

Jade was impressed. "You know Dr. Churn?"

Owens smiled at her expression. "I sure do. She's very articulate, whether in the pulpit or general conversation. A real prayer warrior."

In her interest, Jade forgot she was peeved with the man. "I understand she's been preaching since she was four?"

"She told me so herself."

"Wow, that's amazing!"

"She's an amazing woman. But then, so are you, in your own right."

Jade stared at him. "If you don't mind …"

He slapped his thigh as though a thought had only just then occurred to him. "That's it! You know what I'm going to do? I'm going to introduce one amazing woman to another." Jade's face lit up. "She's going to be our Women's Day speaker and I want you to have dinner with us the day before she preaches, okay?"

"That would be an honor."

"Good, then it's set. Talking about Dr. Churn reminds me of something she told me some years ago. She told me that all unrighteousness is sin, but all sin is not unto death. And when I gave her that same crazy look you're giving me now, she said, look it up for yourself. 1 John 5:17."

"I'll be sure to read it," Jade said mechanically, wondering where this was going.

The pastor nodded owlishly. "I want you to know that I shared a very personal story with Darrell. Now I'm going to tell it to you. I pray that it will help both of you. I'm only doing it because I like you and I don't want you to make the same mistake I did."

Jade said nothing. Her visitor closed his eyes as he spoke. "You see, I've been a sinner from my mother's womb. I never had a chance: none of us does." He lifted his head and looked straight at Jade. "As it says in *Psalms 51:5 Behold, I was shapen in iniquity; and in sin did my mother conceive me.* We … All of us who inhabit this planet … were born in sin. We're wrapped in it." He turned his hands over and lifted his arms. "I call it our earth suit. Better known as the flesh. The problem is we can't live on this planet without it."

"Pastor Owens, I don't understand why …"

"Bear with me for a moment, please." Owens held a hand up and leaned forward in the chair. "I met the love of my life in college. I was a senior finishing up my business degree and she was a freshmen majoring in communications. I loved her from the first day I laid eyes on her. I didn't know it at the time, but she captured my heart. Stole it from the woman I was to marry in less than ten months."

He leaned back again, getting comfortable before continuing. "We started seeing each other regularly, and by Christmas I knew I wanted to marry her. But there was a problem – I'd already asked Nadine Carter to be my wife. Nadine and me, we'd been dating since high school. You see, *her* father was the moderator of the Bethany Baptist Association, and she was headed to medical school on a full scholarship. She was everything a man like me could only dream of." He shook his head, perhaps at the memory. "The Christian community loved Nadine and my parents were crazy about her. I thought I loved Nadine, but it was really just a strong friendship and appreciation for her."

He met Jade's eyes. "You have to understand, I didn't know what love was until I met Cheri Anderson. I told my parents I had met someone and I knew I was in love. They told me to bring her home so they could meet her, check her out, so to speak. I took her to meet my parents two months before I graduated from college. They told me in one hundred different ways how she wasn't the one for me. At first I wasn't hearing them. I wanted to be with Cheri, so I postponed my wedding and planned not to set another date. I didn't want to hurt Nadine, so I told her we needed to wait until she graduated from medical school. I continued to see Cheri regularly – and then Nadine, too, whenever she came home from school. The church folks began to press us to set a new wedding date. I listened to the church folks and I thought about the prestige of being married to a medical doctor and ignored my heart. Mother Evans was the only one who told me, *Boy, you better follow your heart."*

"Sounds just like Mother," Jade acknowledged.

"Yeah, I should have listened to her." He sat back in his seat. "I know you've heard the story about me being caught at the Red Roof Inn with my secretary, Gwen."

It wasn't as if it were a secret. "Who hasn't?"

"Well, the story is partly true. But it wasn't Gwen: it was Cheri I was with." He sighed. "I'd told myself that I couldn't keep living a lie. I needed to practice what I preached and be a real minister of the Lord. So I broke off my affair with Cheri and recommitted myself to God, and for three months I didn't see her." He glanced at Jade. "I won't lie to you. I was in a deep depression over it. But I fasted and I prayed and asked God to remove her from my heart. But no matter how much I prayed or for how long I fasted, she was still ever-present in my heart. But all during that time I never broke down to call her. It was during that time that I found out what Romans 12:1 really meant when it says, *that ye present your bodies a living sacrifice, holy, acceptable unto God* ... Ye meaning I, and it is truly I that has to do that. Anyway ..."

Pastor Owens mind traveled back to the day that became the gossip of the whole church community, the day he'd met Cheri at the Red Roof Inn.

She opened the door before he could knock. "Hello, Preston."

"Cheri." She had gained a few pounds in all the right places. But she was more beautiful than she had been just three months ago. How could that be? He asked himself. "Why did you need to see me?"

"Why don't you come in and close the door." He did as she asked, knowing it was the wrong thing to do. "Have a seat, Preston. I promise I won't touch you unless you want me to," she said with a smile.

His mind told him to leave. Walk away. But no, he took a seat near the desk. "I can't stay. I have a revival going on at the church and I'm in a fast."

"You're fasting? For what?"

"For a closer walk with Him." He pointed to the ceiling.

Cheri looked up. "Do you think He hears people like us, Preston?"

"He hears everyone, Cheri."

"He certainly hasn't heard me. You see, Preston, I've been searching the scriptures for myself and I ran across one that says, and I quote from John 9:31 Now we know that God heareth not sinners: but if any man be a worshipper of God, and doeth his will, him he heareth."

"*Exactly. I've been trying to do His will for the last three months, Cheri. So...*" Owens got up from his chair and started toward the door.

"*I'm getting married, Preston,*" she blurted out.

Owens' hand had just touched the knob on the door and he paused to process what he just heard. "*What? To whom?*" He turned to face her.

"*Curtis Evans.*"

"*Your friend, Curtis?*"

"*Yes.*"

Owens walked over to where she stood and looked into her eyes. He should have been happy for her. Overjoyed, in fact, since he knew he could never leave his marriage. Only death could separate him and Nadine. But he wasn't happy. He was angry and a jealousy he never knew existed rose up inside of him. "*You're lying.*"

"*No, I'm going to marry him. I just wanted to tell you myself.*"

"*You've been sleeping with both of us?*"

"*Now, you know better than that, Preston Owens. I would never lie with one man and then another while...*" she stopped mid-sentence. "*Are you calling me a whore?*"

"*I'm not calling you anything. But if the shoe fits...*"

"*Well, it doesn't fit at all. And how can you judge me? You're no better than I am.*"

Owens stared at her. He didn't want her to marry Curtis. He wanted to marry her. But he couldn't. He had made his bed hard. "*Don't do this just to get back at me.*"

"*If I was going to do something to get back at you, I would have done it when you married Nadine over me.*"

How could he say anything to refute the truth? He couldn't, so he didn't say a word.

"When you walked out on me three months ago, I cried every single day for two weeks. It was Curtis that told me you had an obligation to your family and to the church. I realized that I had no place in your life. We should have separated twelve years ago and then I wouldn't have to be a thirty-four year old woman with no family of my own. So I took Curtis's advice, dried my tears, took myself on a shopping spree and started preparing myself for a future without you. Curtis has always loved me. He wants to give me the family I've always wanted, so I'm going to marry him."

"You love me. How can you be with him when you love me?" he protested.

"The same way you're with Nadine, is how."

"Have you slept with him?"

"That's none of your business, now, is it?"

"I'm going to ask you again. Have you slept with Curtis?" he hissed.

"And I'm going to repeat that it's none of your business."

Owens was silent for a few moments. *"Please, Cheri, just tell me. I need to know if you've been intimate with him?"*

"Would it be easier for you if I said yes, or would it fuel the fire of anger I see in your eyes?"

"I don't know. I only know I need to know if you've been intimate with him."

"You've known me for twelve years, Preston. If you don't know the answer to that question then..."

In one move Owens' hand was around her throat with her back pressed against the wall.

"Go ahead. Do it. Choke the life out of me so I won't have to live in this pain any more. Go on, Preston ... Kill me!"

Owens stared into her eyes and didn't see an ounce of fear, only surprise. "How can I kill you when I love you so much?"

"How can I sleep with Curtis when I love you so much?"

He pressed his lips against hers. The kiss they shared was sinful and passionate, full of lust and love. When their lips parted, Cheri unbuckled his belt and pulled it from the loops. "I don't want to marry Curtis. But I want children. I want a family, Preston." She began to unbutton his shirt. "How can you sleep with her at night and give her babies that should be mine?"

How could he indeed? At that very moment all he knew was that he would be late getting to the church for the revival.

Owens knew he'd told Jade more than he should have. The look on her face was one he'd never seen before. "I didn't mean to be so detailed."

"It's all right. I could tell you were reliving the memory. So tell me, did she get mad at you and rip your clothes up?"

Owens chuckled. "No, she didn't destroy them. After we made love, I fell into a deep sleep. I hadn't had a good night rest in three months. While I was sleeping, she left and took my clothes with her. That is … everything except my shoes."

Jade laughed out loud and so did Owens.

"I called Gwen and asked her to bring one of the suits I keep at the church. She did and it's my understanding Yolanda Payne saw us in the lobby and started the rumor. God knows if I had known it would hurt Gwen the way it did, I wouldn't have called her to help me."

"I wondered why she didn't just leave the church, the way they talked about her."

"Why should she? She hadn't done anything wrong. She only helped me. If she had left then, she would have looked guilty." He shook his head again. "Anyway, Cheri went to the West Jersey Hospital, asked to speak to my wife and gave her my clothes. My wife knew all the time that Gwen had only covered for me. She's always known about Cheri. She just didn't know I was still involved with her."

"But you're still seeing her now?"

"Yes, and that's all I'm willing to tell you about that. But you pray for me. *O wretched man that I am! Who shall deliver me from the body of this death."*

Jade nodded. "Romans 7:24," she said.

"That's right. It goes on to say, *I thank God through Jesus Christ our Lord. So then with the mind I myself serve the law of God, but with the flesh the law of sin.* I love her, Jade. I serve God with my mind and Cheri with my flesh. She's the thorn in my side."

Jade said, shakily, "I want to be holy, Pastor. As holy as I can be, wrapped in this flesh."

"You can. By taking Mother Evans' advice to me. Follow your heart," he responded.

"You don't know who I am. You only see what I want you to see."

"Jade, I think I've been around you enough to know you are a woman after God's own heart. Don't you know that God knows your heart?"

She nodded.

"Then listen to your heart. Don't allow church folks to dictate your life. You allow God to order your steps in his Word. You are free to marry Darrell and I don't think God will be mad at you for doing so. I should have married Cheri. But now, I'm living a life of damnation."

"Darrell doesn't know me, Pastor. He doesn't know who I really am. I've been hiding things about myself from him for years and I don't want him to know about them. I don't want him to know the real me."

"*And ye shall know the truth, and the truth shall make you free.*"

"John 8:32."

"Well, I see you've been studying," he said with a smile.

"I've been quoting that scripture to myself all week," Jade confessed.

"Well, quote it to yourself out loud so your ears can hear the words. Do you know why I say that?"

"I think so, Romans 10:17, *So then faith cometh by hearing, and hearing by the word of God.*"

"You know it." Owens got up and started toward the front door. Jade followed him. "Pray about it, and God will direct your path." Owens stepped out the door.

"Pastor," Jade called to him and he turned to look at her. "Thank you."

He nodded, got in his car and drove away.

CHAPTER EIGHT

On Monday Jade attended classes and talked to her mother about filing a restraining order to keep Keith away from her. She decided to visit the police department after classes. In the meantime, she met Greg in the cafeteria.

"What shakin', Sanders?"

"Hi, Greg. I just *know* you did well on your paper 'cause you're much too cheery to have done otherwise!"

"I made a 95."

She grinned. "Wow, that's great!"

"What can I say, I've got a study partner that makes me think!" He sat down next to her at the table. "You know, Sanders, you really need to think about teaching. You're so good at it."

"You sound like Owens."

"You see, even your pastor, who's rotten to the core, can see you have skills!" he exclaimed.

"He's not my pastor," Jade corrected him. "I just participate in the tutorial program he has at his church."

"So how are your students doing?"

"They're doing great. I couldn't be more proud of them."

"Look at you," Greg said. "Smiling about your kids like you won the million-dollar lottery. You really love those kids. I can see that."

Jade's smile widened. "They make me proud of them."

"No, I think they make you feel good. Yeah, they do. Teaching is your gift, Sanders. You just have a natural talent for it."

"I just happen to have some great kids."

"Uh, Okay. Oh, before I forget … there was a guy here looking for you earlier."

Her stomach tensed. "Looking for me?"

"That's what he said."

Jade looked at him suspiciously. "It wasn't Darrell?"

"I know what Darrell looks like. I've met him twice, remember?"

"Of course I remember." *But I don't want to think about that.*

"Besides, I've never seen this guy before. So I assume he's not a student or with the faculty. Anyway, I told him to check back here in an hour or so."

Her stomach was even tighter now. "Why did you tell him that? You don't even know who this man is!"

He was taken aback. "Yeah, and if he needs to see you, he should do it here, in a public place. At least that's what I thought. I'm not the enemy, Sanders." He stood up. "I'm gonna hit the library. Maybe you can join me later."

"Are you going to be there that long?" She was trying not to sound nervous.

"All of us don't have it like you, Sanders. I have to study twice as hard as you do."

"No you just need to concentrate, I've told you that," she said, the words automatic.

"Well, maybe I suffer from adult attention deficient." Jade's cell phone rang and Greg grabbed it before she could. "Hello."

"Give me my phone, please." Jade snatched it from his hand. "Hello?"

"Jade?"

"Hey, Ashia," she said to her sister. "What's up?"

Greg whispered, "See you later, Sanders."

Jade waved.

"I need you to talk to Mommy for me."

Jade sighed. "What's going on now?"

"I want to go to Teresa's party Friday night."

"Ashia, why do you always try to get me involved in yours and Mom's disagreements? I can't override her decisions! You know that, and you know how she is."

"But she listens to you, Jade, please just talk to her. I really want to go. Everybody's gonna be there."

"Everybody? What kind of party is it, anyway?"

"It's a house party for her birthday. Then, there's gonna be a pajama party for ten of her best friends and I'm one of them."

"Does Mom know her parents?"

"No, but they're good people."

"Uh-huh." *That's what they all say*, she thought.

"Come on, Jade."

"Ashia, I've told you and told you, Mom's job is to protect you from all hurt, harm and danger. She's going to want to know where your friend's parents work, and everything. You know how she is."

"Jade," she whined, "you don't understand. She won't let me do anything. It's like she don't trust me."

"It's not you she doesn't trust, it's all the other people. Believe me, Ashia, you'll be grateful she loved you enough to shelter you from these crazy people out here in this big bad world."

"She won't even let me go to the mall in broad daylight without supervision! I'm not a baby anymore. I'm almost fifteen years old." There was silence between them. "Please talk to her, Jade. She has me locked down like a prisoner."

Jade laughed at the comment. "I think you're exaggerating a bit." She was vaguely aware of someone stopping and standing next to her.

"This ain't funny, Jade."

Jade tilted her head back to see who was standing there, and the laughter died on her lips. "Let me call you back, okay?"

"You'll talk to Mom for me?"

"Yeah … I'll call you back," Jade answered without hearing Theashia's question.

"Hello, Jade. It's been a long time."

It was Keith Strickland.

Jade's stomach contracted. She couldn't believe he was pursuing her. She couldn't believe that he was here on campus.

"You're even more beautiful than I remember. Maturity has really brought out the best in you."

Jade didn't reply. She began gathering her books together to make her exit. Her stomach was churning again.

"Look, Jade, I just need to ask you a few questions. Just listen. I promise you won't have to communicate with me anymore."

"I don't want you to ask me any questions," she snapped, not looking at him. "I asked you to leave me alone." She began pushing her books into her bag.

"Please, I'm not here to cause you distress."

"Well, you sure have fooled me!"

"I just want to know what agency did the adoption."

Jade looked around the noisy cafeteria and was glad she hardly knew anyone. "This is not the time or the place."

"You tell me when and where and I'll be there."

"Why don't you try ten o'clock?"

"I can do ten."

"In the year 2099." Jade made her exit.

Keith followed behind her. "Jade, please. This really means a lot to me."

Jade continued out the building, heading for her car.

"Jade, wait!"

Jade spotted her car and quickened her pace.

"Why won't you just give me whatever information you have?"

"You had your chance over sixteen years ago." Jade continued to walk quickly and Keith speeded up, closing the distance between them. "When you signed away your rights, you knew it was forever. You have to live with that decision the same way I have to live with mine." When she reached her car, she pushed the black button to unlock the door. "Now I'm going to ask you again to please leave me alone and don't attempt to contact me again."

"I made a mistake. I need to make amends."

Jade got into her car and closed the door. "It's too late for that."

He leaned closer to her window. "It's never too late unless one of us is dead."

"Hopefully, you'll never know. Now, I'm begging you to stay away from me." She started the car and pulled away, leaving Keith standing in the middle of the parking lot scratching his head.

Jade was nervous. She couldn't remember being so panicked in all her life. Keith had unnerved her and she didn't know how to handle it. "Jesus, Jesus, Jesus," she said, hitting the steering wheel each time she prayed His name. "Why can't he just leave me alone?" When a horn from another car blew, she knew she needed to pull the car over to regain her composure.

She pulled over in the PathMark supermarket parking lot. "Breathe, Jade. Breathe slowly," she cautioned herself. "What am I going to do? Oh, God, what am I going to do?" She knew her mother wasn't home, so she tried her cell number but there was no answer. She sat in the parking lot for almost twenty minutes, then punched in her friend's number. She prayed she was home. "Answer your phone, please answer your phone."

"Hello?"

"Ivy, oh thank God, you're home. Thank God. I'm on my way to your house."

"Okay, I'm here. You sound funny. You all right?

"No."

"What's wrong? Why aren't you at school?"

"I'm done with all my classes for today. I'll see you in a few, okay?"

"All right. Drive safe."

಄಍಄

When Ivy opened the door for Jade, her friend greeted her with a firm hug and immediately burst into tears. Ivy had never seen Jade unglued before. She hardly ever let her emotions show, and Ivy was caught off guard by the outburst. Nevertheless, Ivy immediately wrapped her arms around Jade and they stood at the door as Ivy held her, stoking her back as she cried uncontrollably.

Jade attempted to get herself under control, but the tears kept flowing. She needed to talk to someone other than God. She trusted Ivy more than any of her friends; and now she needed to talk about things Ivy had been longing to know for years.

"Come on in here. You okay?" Ivy stepped back and took a real good look at Jade. "I could tell by the sound of your voice you're terribly troubled."

"Did you pray for me like I asked?" Jade asked as she tried to dry her tears.

"You know I did. What's going on?"

"Can I have something to drink?"

"Juice, coffee, tea?"

"I need a real drink." Ivy looked at her as if she had lost her mind. "I know you have hot chocolate," Jade amended.

"Yes, that I have. Come on."

Jade followed Ivy into her spacious kitchen. "Where are the kids?"

Ivy looked at the clock on her wall. "Well, it's five o'clock, so they're probably with Bill at the arcade. Bill gets them every Wednesday and they hang out and eat junk food."

"They've been spending a lot of time with him."

"Uh-uh, you're not changing the subject. Talk to me, what's going on?"

"What I'm about to tell you, I want kept between you and me. I don't want you to discuss it with anyone, not your mother, not your father, not Randi or Sheena. Not anybody."

"Dang, girl, you haven't killed anyone, have you?"

"I'm serious, Ivy. I really need you to say it will remain between me and you."

"Okay." Ivy pointed between the two of them. "You and me. Right here."

"Promise me."

"Didn't I just say it stays right here?"

"Promise me, Ivy."

"All right, I promise. I won't breathe a word to a soul."

Jade let out a long breath of relief. "You know how everyone wants to know what went on with me before I moved here?"

"You mean when you first came here from North Carolina?"

"Yes."

Ivy nodded. "Go on, I'm listening." She sat down at the table.

"Well, my past just caught up with me." Jade paused. "About two weeks ago, I got a phone call from Keith Strickland."

"Who's that?"

"Keith and I had a relationship before I came to live here." Jade dropped her chin to her chest. "We had a child together."

Ivy's mouth dropped open but she didn't say anything.

"We both signed papers giving the baby up for adoption. I never wanted anyone to know. But Keith is determined to find the child and I don't want him to."

Ivy didn't know what to say. The buzzer from the microwave snapped her out of her daze.

"When I came here, I had every intention of living an ordinary life with ordinary people. But when I started school I met Darrell."

Ivy pushed the cup of hot chocolate in front of Jade and sat down again in the chair across from her at the table.

"When we moved here my mother told me to concentrate on school so I could go to college and be everything that the people in my old neighborhood said I'd never be." Jade paused. "I know just how evil people can be. Just how words can hurt a person. Even kill their dreams. When my mother saw just how badly the talk was affecting me emotionally, she and my dad decided to move to another state. It was my father who told me if anyone asks me about my past to simply say, *I had no life before I came here*." She looked up and met Ivy's eyes. "You will *never* know how many times I wanted to tell you about my past. I'm sitting here right now debating just how much to tell you." Jade began twisting her ring.

No way was Ivy going to interrupt her train of thought. She sat quietly and listened to her friend.

"Anyway, I never told anyone about the baby. My mother and father were the only ones who knew everything. My mother told me to keep it that way so I could have a second chance.

Jade took a deep breath. "I soon found out that once you awaken your flesh to sexual activity, it's not easy just turning it off. God knows I've been trying for years. Some days I struggle more than others to control the sensational craving I get sometimes."

Ivy chuckled. "I know exactly what you mean. It's been a struggle for me since Ray died. I'm definitely a woman who needs to be married!"

Jade gave Ivy a sad smile. "You know that line in *The Color Purple* when Celie's father tells Mister she's been spoiled twice? Well, that's me, spoiled twice." Jade stood up and walked over to the window, looking out at Ivy's unfinished garden. "I see the gazebo is almost done."

"Yeah, hopefully the whole thing will be done in the spring."

Jade turned to Ivy. "It's going to be beautiful."

Ivy knew Jade was attempting to end her confession and she wasn't having it. "So what're you going to do?"

"Good question." What could she do? "I want to go to a place where no one knows me so I can start all over again."

"You've been there, done that."

Jade leaned against the counter. "Yeah, I know."

"You need to come clean with Darrell. He loves you. He'll understand."

"No way. I'm never telling him!" Jade came back to the table and sat down across from Ivy. "I just need a few months. I want to finish school so I can move to Tampa and just get away from here."

"Jade, be sensible."

"I'm trying to be sensible, Ivy." Jade began twisting her ring. "I don't want Darrell to be embarrassed because of the things I've done. I don't want my son to know what I did, either."

"Look, if you just be honest with Darrell and tell him the same way you're telling me now and allow…"

"No! I'd rather die than for him to find out."

"Okay … calm down." Ivy had never seen Jade like this before.

"I'm scared, Ivy."

Ivy placed her hands over Jade's. "Fear is not of God."

"Yeah, I know, and He don't bless mess either, and my life's loaded with it."

"Jade, just hear me out for a moment. For almost two years you had the man's son and didn't tell him. He found out and continued to love you anyway."

"That's the next thing. Knowing all I've done why does he still want to be bothered with me? I mean, why can't he just move on with his life?"

"It's called love, Jade. The man's in love with you, I can't understand for the life of me why you can't understand that."

"I don't deserve his love."

"Well, we don't deserve God's love either, but He loves us in spite of ourselves. That's the kind of love Darrell has for you."

She shook her head. "I don't want him to love me, Ivy. I just want to finish school and move out of this state." Jade blew out her breath in frustration. "Darrell's always there. He makes excuses to come there late at night, *like I'm just checking on you and Dee,* when he knows Medford has the safest neighborhood in New Jersey."

"He just wants to be around you, Jade. I've been telling you that."

"He's a tease, Ivy. He likes to provoke and tempt me. It's wrong. It's so bad that I can hardly sleep at night."

"That's love you feel."

"That's lust I feel."

"If it were lust, it wouldn't matter who you were with. You'd just satisfy the craving with anyone available. Do you do that?"

"No!"

"Then I think it's safe to say it's not lust you're feeling, it's love." Ivy grasped her friend's hand. "Tell him how you feel. Be open and honest with him." Ivy paused. "I know how much he cares for you and I'd be willing to guarantee that he won't judge you.

"He's going to be disappointed," Jade whispered.

"If he is, he'll get over it."

CHAPTER NINE

Keith sat in his car debating whether he should knock on the door of Jade's parents' home.

The restraining order delivered to him the day before had only said not to go near Jade or the house in which she lived. He was also restricted from going onto the Rutgers campus. However, it never said anything about her parents' home.

Keith got out of the car, hoping he could make Mrs. Sanders understand his position. He needed to find his child. The search was imperative, because he knew he would never father another. Just before he graduated from college he'd been diagnosed with testicular cancer, and the treatment made fatherhood impossible. The older he got, the more he wanted to know about the child he'd given up all those years ago.

He confirmed the address on the paper again, approached the door and knocked.

A teenage girl answered and Keith smiled at her.

"Hi, can I help you?" she asked.

"Yes, I'm looking for Mrs. Nora Sanders. Is she here?"

"No, I'm sorry; she's not home."

"Who is it, Paula?" a voice from within the house asked.

"It's somebody for your mother," she called back, then turned back to him. "I'm sorry, what's your name?"

"Keith Strickland."

Keith's eyes widened when he saw the girl who came up behind Paula. He stared at her and whispered, "Jade."

The girl stepped in front of Paula, giving Keith a good view of her.

"I'm not Jade! I'm her sister. My name's Theashia."

It took a moment for Keith to collect himself. He stammered, "Theashia! Wow. That's an unusual name … but it's very pretty."

Theashia smiled. "Unusual. You may be right about that! I'm the only Theashia I know."

"You must be much younger that Jade, 'cause you weren't around when your family lived in North Carolina."

"Well, we moved right after I was born."

"You're what … Thirteen?"

"Close enough, fourteen. I'll be fifteen on the twenty-fourth of next month."

A car pulled in the driveway and the door opened. "Here's my mom now. Hi, Mommy!" she yelled.

"Hey, you and Paula come and help me with these bags," she called back.

Both girls went to the car to help take the groceries in the house.

"I told you girls no company, didn't I?"

"We didn't have any company, Mrs. Sanders," said Paula virtuously.

She frowned. "Then who's that man at the door?"

"He's not here for us! He's here for you!" Theashia protested.

"For me?" She narrowed her eyes but didn't recognize the man standing by the door. "I don't know him." Keith started toward her car.

"He said his name is Keith Something," Paula said before heading toward the house with her grocery bags.

Keith was standing by the car now. "Hello, Mrs. Sanders. It's been a long time."

"Go in the house, Ashia," she snapped.

"What's wrong, Mommy?"

"Don't ask me any questions. You and Paula go in the house right now. Go and call the police."

Theashia hurried in behind Paula.

Keith made placating gestures with his hands. "Mrs. Sanders, please: that isn't necessary."

"Oh, yes, it is. You're trespassing on private property and there's a restraining order against you."

"I only want to talk to you, just let me …"

She interrupted him sharply. "Get off my property right now!"

"Please, Mrs. Sanders, I won't …"

"Get off my property *now*!" she shouted.

Theashia appeared in the doorway. "The police are on the way," she announced.

"Don't come out here," Nora commanded her. "Get back in the house."

"Please," Keith begged.

She didn't even look at him as she stalked into the house, slamming the door behind her.

Keith got into his car and drove away.

ഇൗരു

Jade never lifted her head from the book she was reading when Keith walked into her classroom at the church. Even after he approached her, she didn't move, she was so engrossed.

"Jade."

Jade looked up and did a double take when she saw it was Keith. "What are you doing here?" She looked around the room. "Who let you in?"

"I saw her, Jade." His voice was raspy and his nostrils flared. "I saw my daughter."

Jade sat back in her chair. "What?"

"I saw her. She looks just like you."

Slowly, Jade realized what he meant. She drew in a deep breath and didn't say anything.

"You've had her all this time. You never gave her away, after all," he said brokenly. "I went to your parents' house. Her name's Theashia. She's beautiful."

"Oh, my God." She whispered the words.

"Why didn't you just tell me you had her?"

Jade was suddenly angry. She glared at him. "You've been served with an order to stay away from me."

"Damn the order. You need to talk to me about why you didn't want me to know where she was."

"I don't care to talk to you. I thought I made that plain the last time we spoke."

He refused to let her change the subject. "She doesn't know anything, does she? You never told her who she really is."

"She knows all she needs to know," Jade snapped.

"Well, she'll know more, once I talk to her."

Jade slammed her fist on the table. "You want to destroy her? Why would you want to hurt her?"

"That's crazy."

"Is it? You're upset because I stuck around to be sure she received the best? You just let her go. I'm the one who made provision for her to have a good life!"

"I just want to get to know her, Jade. I'm her father! I have the same rights that you have."

"No, you don't. You made the decision to walk away. *I* stayed around and toughed it out when *you* chose to walk away fifteen years ago."

Keith ran his hands over his baldhead and blew out a sigh. "I know I made the wrong decision."

"So, now that's my fault? Or Theashia's fault?"

"No," he hesitated. "Let's not talk about faults, Jade. She's a part of me. That alone gives me some rights."

She wasn't listening to the pain in his voice, only to his words. And perhaps her own pain. "You don't have any rights. Don't you see? I don't have any rights, either! I didn't raise her. I didn't provide for her. When she had the chicken pox, I was too busy doing my undergraduate work. I wasn't at her first school play, or at her baptism." She took a deep, shuddering breath. "But my parents *were*. To her, they are her mother and father. They love her, and she loves them. Yes, I decided who would raise her. Yes, I handpicked them. And I picked the very best. She never knew she was rejected. She never knew you didn't want her."

Jade stood up and stood directly in front of him. "So don't you give me this crap about having rights."

Jade saw Mother Brown entering the room. But she was letting herself vent anger she'd held in for a long time. "You have some nerve to even show your face, after all these years!"

"Jade," Mother Brown called gently, and Jade looked at her. "I told your mother that this man was here. She told me to call the police, so I did."

Two men had followed her into the room; now approaching Jade. She held up her hand. "Deacon Walker, Brother Payne, it's all right. Keith was just leaving."

Keith said, helplessly, "Jade …"

She turned to him. "Don't allow your wants to be above her needs. I'm begging you, Keith. Please, if you have any compassion, please, leave her alone. Now is not the time. Not while she's still so young."

Keith stood there a moment. He looked over at the two men standing near Mother Brown. Brother Payne pointed to the door. "The exit is this way, my brother." Deacon Walker opened it wide and waited for Keith to leave. When he left, the men followed. Mother Brown stayed where she was. "You all right, Jade?"

Jade couldn't answer. Her carefully constructed world was tumbling around her. Now everyone would know. Her mind was spinning. "Oh, God! Oh God!" She covered her face with both hands as her body began to shake violently.

Mother Brown rushed to her side and wrapped the sobbing Jade in her arms.

"I'm so sorry, Mother."

"It's all right, baby. Cryin' is good for the soul. It cleanses ya."

"Then I should be good and clean, for all the crying I've been doing for the last few weeks!"

Mother Brown smiled. "Here, take my tissues."

Jade felt ashamed of herself. Now Mother Brown knew about her biggest secret. "I never wanted anyone to know, Mother."

"Just so you know, I still don't know. Deacon Walker and Brother Payne, they don't know, neither."

"Oh, Mother!" A wave of gratitude engulfed Jade.

She took her chin to raise her head. "That's the way it stays till you say different."

CHAPTER TEN

Mother Brown asked Deacon Walker to follow Brother Payne as he drove Jade home.

Jade was quiet during the fifteen-minute drive, turning the situation over and over again in her mind. No matter how she played out the scenario, the conclusion was the same. *I have to tell Darrell.* She couldn't risk him finding out any other way.

Brother Payne walked Jade to the door. "You going to be all right?"

"Yes, thank you."

"Do you need anything before we go?" Deacon Walker's car idled in the driveway behind him as he spoke.

"No, thank you."

He nodded. "Why don't you call one of your friends to come over and sit with you for a while?"

Jade shook her head. "Thank you for seeing me home. I know it was an inconvenience and I …"

"Don't be silly. I'd do it again."

Jade gave him a weak smile and nodded.

"Take care. See you tomorrow."

When Jade closed the door behind him, she thought, *how am I going to tell Darrell? When?*

Now. She walked into her bedroom, sat on the side of the bed and dialed Darrell's number. He answered on the first ring.

"Hey, baby."

"I need to see you," she said curtly.

Darrell paused. *Something's wrong*, he thought. "When, now?"

"In an hour, if that's all right." Her heart was thudding in her chest.

His voice was quizzical. "Okay, sure, see you then."

She was about to hang up when she remembered something. "Darrell."

"Yeah?"

"Can you ask your mother if Dee can sleep over tonight? I'd really rather talk with you alone."

"No problem."

When Jade hung up she wanted to cry. She didn't want to face Darrell. But there was no way she would allow him to find out from Keith – or anyone else for that matter. He deserved better than that: she had no choice. This had to be done.

ဧာ၈ာ

When Darrell arrived, the house was dark. Only the lights in the family room were on. "Jade!" he called out to her as he let himself in.

"I'm in here."

Jade was sitting near the window. Outside, it had begun snowing. "If I'd known about the snow I wouldn't've asked you to come out."

"It's all right. I could tell that it's important." Darrell walked over and brushed the back of her hand with his fingertips.

"That little tree is still holding on," she said nostalgically, looking out at the lawn below where the baby oak tree she and Darrell had planted the summer before still stood, supported by ropes tied to the ground.

Darrell looked out the window. "Yeah, it's weathered the heat and now it's holding on through the cold." He paused, giving Jade the space to lead into whatever it was she had to say to him. After a while he asked, "What's the problem, baby?"

Jade turned and gazed at him for a moment, regretting already what she was about to say and do. But it was something she had to do for the sake of everyone concerned. *Oh, if this bitter cup could pass* ... She prayed there could have been another way out of this forest.

Darrell pulled her close to him. "What's wrong?" When he lifted his hand to touch her face, she moved away. He dropped his hand and his eyes filled with worry.

"I need to tell you something." She took a deep breath. I need to tell you *everything*." She stood up, walked over to the piano, and sat down on the bench. "I've been debating where to start and I guess I need to start at the beginning."

Darrell came closer to her. "Good place to start." He leaned on the piano.

"I want to say what I have to say and I don't want you to say a word. I just need to tell my story without interruption, okay?"

Darrell sat down next to her. "Okay."

Jade got up and walked to the window again. She didn't want to be so close to him. Just thinking about the disappointment her deception was going to cause him was enough. She didn't want to see it in his eyes.

She folded her arms across her chest, took a deep breath and began. "I wasn't born Jade Marie Sanders." She looked at him for a moment then continued. "I was born Jade Marie Smith." She paused for a reaction. None came. He was respecting her request for silence. "My birth mother's name is Maxine Smith. I barely knew her when she died." She gave a sad smile as a memory flashed in her mind.

"Who's that, Grand Matilda?"

"That's your mommy, baby. You remember Max, don't you?"

Five-year old Jade looked down at the body dressed in white, lying in the coffin. She remembered the name, but that didn't look like the person she knew as Max.

"I didn't recognize my own mother lying in a casket." Jade sighed and looked down at the floor. "The only memory I have of her was the day she took me out to get ice cream. We were having a great time that day. The next thing I knew, Grand Matilda, picked me up and took me out of there. I knew they were arguing, but I didn't know why. I understood after I got older that she didn't want me around her because she was in an abusive relationship with her pimp."

Jade looked at Darrell again for a reaction, but what she saw was unreadable. She pressed on. "My grandmother wasn't saved, and we didn't go to church or anything like that. She was the numbers lady." Jade began to twist the ring on her finger. "I used to give people numbers from the dream book that my grandmother kept in the kitchen cabinet. On weekends people came to our house to drink and gamble."

Jade paused and Darrell could tell she was thinking. So he waited, listening intently, not wanting to miss a single word.

"Come to think of it, that's probably why I'm so good with numbers." She looked at Darrell and he gave her a soft smile. "I think that's how she made money. I don't remember her working or doing anything other than that." Jade paused to think about that for a moment. "When I was about eight or nine, I asked my grandmother about my father. She told me that she didn't know who he was. She said my mother never told anyone." She shrugged. "Could be that my mother didn't know who he was. Unlike our son, my features never gave me away. I look just like my mother, who looks just like her mother," Jade turned to look out the window again. She took a deep breath. "And my daughter looks just like me."

"Your daughter?" There was sharp surprise in Darrell's voice.

Jade nodded her head as her eyes filled with tears.

Darrell stood up. "Jade, what –"

"Please!" she turned to him and held up her hand to stop his movement and words. "Just let me finish!"

"I'm sorry."

"Where was I?" She looked around her, a little lost. "Oh, my father. I have no idea who he is. I only know that somebody told my grandmother that it was a man named Glen Thompson. But when my grandmother died, social services contacted him. Blood test proved I wasn't his." Jade went to the sofa to sit. She was still unable to relax.

"Every day of school, my grandmother would walk me to and from the bus stop. On the day she didn't show up to get me, I knew something was wrong. When I got to the house I went to the kitchen. There lay my grandmother on the floor – in a pool of blood. I should have realized she was dead, but I couldn't imagine a woman who was so big being dead."

Darrell asked, pain filling his voice, "What happened?"

"She was stabbed to death by a guy who played a number. He thought he was being cheated out of his winnings. Come to find out, the woman who played the number for him kept the winnings for herself." Jade began twisting her ring again. "When the police finally came, I was on the floor with her head in my lap." Jade looked over at Darrell. "They gave the guy ten years for manslaughter. It's my understanding he only did six of those ten years. Good behavior. Six years for a life." Sarcasm tinged her voice. "That's justice for you."

She didn't like thinking about her Grand Matilda. It always made her cry. "When he killed my grandmother, he destroyed something inside me. I've never been able to recover from it." Jade was in pain from trying to keep from crying. "I was ten years old. No family. Nowhere to go. So the state placed me in foster care. The first year I was in the system I lived in six different homes. I just couldn't adjust."

Darrell wanted to hold her, but he dared not move. He was finally getting the information he'd been asking for. The more he heard, the more he understood her.

"I met Alan and Nora Sanders when I was in the care of Frank and Doris Pratt. They lived right next door. For the first time since my grandmother died, I felt cared for. By then my grandmother had been gone two years. I used to hang out at the Sanders', because they had a foster child named Lisa living with them. Lisa and I became good friends."

She twisted her ring some more. "I just wanted to belong. That's what all this was about. Well, the boy across the street made me feel … special. I was twelve when I met him. His name was Keith Strickland. He was fifteen."

Jade took a deep breath. "All the girls in the neighborhood had a crush on him. But he liked me. Yeah, I thought that was real special. Because of Keith, I didn't want to move anymore. I wanted to be sure that I was obedient and useful so they wouldn't want to send me away." Jade laughed at the memory. "I did everything I could to please Mary Pratt. I thought if I did that, she would want to keep me forever." She sighed. "So I cooked. I cleaned. I made sure she never had to scold me for anything."

She shrugged. "Then Lisa went back home to her family. I knew that going back home would be the worse thing for her. Since we couldn't see each other, we talked on the phone every day. Then one day I called and asked to speak to her and they told me she was gone. At first no one would tell me what happened to her. But the murder was on television. She was beaten to death by her mother's boyfriend."

Jade stood and went to the window. She couldn't keep still. "It took me a long time to get over her death. Anyway, after Lisa died, Doris Pratt's mother became ill. She began spending a lot of time in Dallas. So she left me with the Sanders. That was just fine with me, because I didn't want to spend any time away from Keith. I thought I was in love." She shrugged again. "Then the Pratts moved back to Texas. I thank God every day, you know, for Alan and Nora Sanders. They were able to get me placed with them and immediately after that they started adoption procedures. I started calling them Mama and Daddy soon as they told me they wanted to adopt me."

She wasn't making any eye contact with Darrell. She couldn't. She just wanted to finish, now that she'd started.

"Keith and I became closer and I allowed him to have liberties with me that I shouldn't have. By the time the adoption went through we were inseparable. About a year later I found myself pregnant. I knew it would disappoint my mother. I should have listened to her. Anyway, when Keith's family found out, they weren't pleased. He signed away all his rights to the child and severed all ties with me."

She stretched and sighed. "My pregnancy caused such a stir in the neighborhood that it forced us to move. We went to Stone Mountain, Georgia, first. That's where Theashia was born. I was sixteen. Way too young. I was going to give her up for adoption, but... I just couldn't do it. I just couldn't be as heartless as Keith. I couldn't give my baby to strangers. So... I asked my mom and dad to adopt her." She smiled through her tears. "They never wanted me to give the child away. They were willing to help me raise the baby and just be proud grandparents. But I wanted them to have her! I wanted her to have a mother and a father. I wanted her to have a family. So... I gave up my rights as a parent, but I knew I'd always be in her life this way. And then we moved to New Jersey, and you know the rest."

Darrell finally spoke. "So Theashia is totally in the dark? She doesn't know anything?"

"No. And she doesn't need to know right now."

"So if you didn't see this Keith guy after that, then why did I take a call from him the other day?"

"I *hadn*'t seen him. Not for years. But right after Christmas he got in touch with me." Jade told him everything that had happened after Keith found her. "Hopefully the restraining order will keep him away from Theashia. Mom and I have been thinking about telling her the truth."

Jade pulled out the large envelope she had laying on the end table and handed it to Darrell. "This envelope has all the documentation you need to take over full custody of Desmond. Shot records, birth certificate, and Social Security card. Bill Hart can help you with filing for legal custody and I'll sign whatever is necessary."

Darrell was staring at Jade in total disbelief.

Jade didn't care anymore about the tears falling. This was something she dreaded doing. She never wanted to give her son away to anyone. "Raise him right, Darrell. Give him what your parents gave you." She attempted to wipe her eyes; she couldn't see past the tears. "The keys to your house are in there as well." She pointed at the envelope in his hand. "I want to thank you for being so good to me."

Darrell stood up and headed toward her. "Jade …" She backed away while shaking her head. Darrell stopped. "Why are you doing this?"

"I'm doing what's best for my son."

"You think him being without you is best for him?"

"He's still young. He'll adjust."

Darrell was confused. Shaking his head he whispered her name. "Jade… baby…"

She had to ignore the plea she heard in his voice. The last thing she wanted was sympathy. After a story like that, she knew he would feel sorry for her, and she didn't want his pity. She fought to keep her voice steady. "If it's all right with you, I'd like to get Desmond two weeks in the summer, and every other Christmas. I'd like to come and see him whenever I can – at your discretion, of course." Jade walked over to the chair, picked up her jacket and headed for the front door.

"Where are you going?" Darrell followed her.

"I'm leaving. I've said all I needed to say."

Jade pulled the door open to escape.

"Oh, no, you don't." Darrell was at the door next to her and pushed it shut. "You're not going to tell me what you had to say, then walk out on me."

"I think I've said everything that's needed to be said."

"But I haven't had a chance to say anything."

"I've given you everything." She cried. "You have your son, your house, everything… You're free."

He leaned toward her. "No, I don't have everything. I still don't have you."

She met his eyes. "I'm no good for you. I come from bad… bad seed. You'll never know how many times I prayed and asked God to make me worthy. I wish I had a tenth of your integrity."

"You've always underestimated yourself."

She shook her head. "You deserve more than I could ever give you."

"You are everything I want, everything I need." He touched her face, gently, tentatively.

"Oh, Darrell … How can you still want…"

"You had your say, now it's my turn." Darrell took her by the hand and headed back to the family room. "Sit down." At first she didn't comply. "Please."

When she did, he sat next to her on the sofa taking both her hands in his. "Seems to me you've been protecting everyone. Me, Dee, Theashia. But who's protecting Jade? Who's looking out for Jade?"

"I don't need protection."

"I see it differently. You've done things your way. Well, now it's time to do it my way."

"You didn't hear me did you? You don't have to…"

"My way, Jade." He steadied his voice. "I have one question for you. You have to be totally honest with me, okay?" She nodded. "You really do love me, right?"

"Yes, but love..."

"Then you're going to marry me. I'm not asking you, I'm telling you." Jade's jaw slacked; she was astonished.

"I can't marry you."

"Why?" He paused for an answer. "You love me. I love you. We already started a family."

"I can't be a minister's wife."

"Why?" He was stern.

"I just can't pretend to be something that I'm not."

"What are you?"

Jade looked at him not answering.

"I'll tell you what you are. You're a survivor. You were dealt a hard hand and you won against all the odds." Darrell lifted her hand and kissed it. "Now, what you have to do is forgive yourself for everything that's happened in the past. I had to forgive myself too, Jade." Darrell touched her chin so he could tilt her head to look into his eyes. "Did you know that God forgives us as soon as we ask?" Jade nodded. "So why are you holding on to it? Why are you punishing yourself?"

Jade had no reply because she had no answer.

"Let me ask you something, do babies have a past?"

"No," she sniffled.

"Neither do born-again believers. When you become born again, you become a babe in Christ. Babes have no past. You are a new creature."

Jade gave a little smile. She'd never thought of it that way before.

"When you asked for forgiveness, God threw it into a sea of forgetfulness to never be thought of again. So, the only time God remembers it is when you remind Him of it."

She nodded. "I'm finished with it."

That made Darrell smile. "Now that we've got that out the way, we're going to get married."

Jade stared at him without a challenge.

"I'll arrange everything."

Jade lowered her eyes. "I don't know, I... –"

He took her hand. "It's going to be all right. So don't worry."

She nodded her agreement, still in awe of everything.

Darrell cleared his throat. "As for Mr. Strickland, I'm going to have a little talk with him. Do you know where to find him?"

"No." She blew out a sigh. "I'm sorry."

"Don't worry about it. It's mine to handle now. Call your mother and tell all your friends: we're getting married."

"Are you sure? I mean, maybe you should wait. Allow yourself to absorb everything I just told you."

He took both her hands and looked directly into her face. "I know what you're thinking. But let me assure you: I want to marry you, and only you. I'm not trying to marry your mother, your father, your grandmother, or anyone else in your family. All I want is you. That's all."

A tremendous sense of relief swept over Jade. It was like a bright light had illuminated all the dark places inside her. She relaxed, and when she did, she sobbed and sobbed. Darrell pulled her into his arms and whispered loving words to console her.

She leaned back to look up at him. "I'm so sorry for everything."

"It's all right, baby. We're not going to talk about it anymore. So stop crying."

"But I'm happy. I can't help it."

Darrell pulled her closer to him. "Then cry all you want to."

They sat there, with no words passing between them. Jade held him tight. *It's all over*, she thought. *Thank you, God, it's all over.* Jade pressed as close to Darrell as she could.

After a long while Darrell felt her relaxing her hold. He looked into her eyes smiled and kissed her on the forehead. He got up, went to the phone on the other side of the room and pressed in a number. Jade never took her eyes off him.

"Good evening, Pastor Jones, I'd like to see you if I can, sir." Short pause. "Yes, sir, it's an emergency."

CHAPTER ELEVEN

The room was so silent anyone could have heard a pen drop. Jade didn't know what to expect and all eyes were on her. She scanned each of her friend's faces one by one watching the expression on each. Miranda, Sheena and Ivy were all stunned. Jade dropped her eyes to the floor. *Maybe they weren't ready to know everything all at once,* she thought.

Finally, Miranda said, "Now, let me see if I'm understanding you correctly. Your mother and your father are not your mother and father. And … your sister is not your sister. And … you're getting married?"

Jade nodded.

"Theashia doesn't know? Sheena asked.

"No, and I don't want her to. Not yet."

Silence again.

Jade roused herself. "Look, I know all this is shocking to you all. You may even be upset with me for deceiving you." She paused. "You all have been my friends since I came here." She sniffled. "I just hope that you'll continue to …"

Before she could finish her sentence, Sheena sprang from her seat, encircled her arms around Jade and squeezed her tight. "You know we're in shock. But we still love you, you silly woman."

"Ah, I think Jade needs a group hug!" Ivy announced.

They stood in the middle of the floor, all four women hugging each other. Jade couldn't hold back the tears any longer. But, they were joyous.

When they separated, Sheena asked, "So when's the wedding?"

"I don't know." Jade wiped her eyes. "But it won't be anything big. Probably just Darrell and me −" she looked at Ivy "− in your father's study." Pastor Jones was the senior pastor of Cathedral of Faith, and Ivy's father.

"I assume Darrell don't want to wait one more minute than he has to," Sheena joked.

Jade chuckled. "If Darrell had his way it would have been done yesterday."

All the women laughed.

"You're gonna laugh when I say this. But do you know what I thought about you and your past?"

"What?"

"I thought you were in the witness protection program."

Jade did laugh; and so did everyone else. "Really?"

Miranda nodded. "Well, what did you expect? You kept telling us you had no past. So I just thought you and your family had been relocated by the federal government."

"It made sense to me. But, anyway, where is Theashia's father?" Sheena asked

"I hadn't seen him since way before I had her. Then about a month ago he called me." Jade told them about the first phone call to the last meeting at the church.

"Looks like you're going to need a lawyer. And I know the perfect man for you, too." Sheena paused. "Vincent Marshall."

"Oh, you mean Bill's friend?" Jade asked.

Sheena nodded. "The man is good. Real good."

Miranda had a question. "So you had to give up your rights so that your parents could adopt Theashia?"

"No, I didn't have to do that. I wanted it that way. They were willing to help me raise her and be grandparents. I thought it was best if they adopted her. So my dad found an attorney who took care of the paperwork, and I know it was the best thing to do."

"Well, if anyone can help you, Marshall can. He's the best when it comes to family law. But watch out: he's expensive. He loves money and he loves making it."

"The love of money is the root of all evil," Miranda commented.

"Well, you're going to need evil to deal with evil." Sheena replied.

"That may be so, but right now I'm hungry." Miranda laughed and headed for the kitchen.

"See, that's why you can't lose any weight. All you think about is food," Ivy said. "And don't worry about money, Jade. I got your back."

"I think about more things than food. As a matter of fact, I've been thinking about Sheena a whole lot lately."

"Why are you thinking about me?"

"Jason called me to find out how you were doin'."

She stopped and stared. "He called you?"

"Actually, he just didn't come out and say, I'm calling about Sheena. He said he was calling to get José's phone number."

"He knows José's number."

"Yeah, I know. I told him so after he said, *by the way, how's Sheena.*"

They settled themselves in Ivy's kitchen for an extended girl talk.

"Now that we know why Jade didn't want to commit to Darrell, I think it's time for you to tell us why you ran Jason to another state, Ms. Thing." Ivy reached into the refrigerator and removed a fruit salad.

Miranda opened the cabinet, retrieving some bowls. "Who wants a bowl to eat something … hum … healthy?"

"Don't be funny. Just give everyone a bowl, Rugrat," Ivy responded.

"I didn't run him to another state. He left because he wanted to leave."

"Sheena, all of us know that Jason is your IBM. So why are you trippin'?" Miranda cut in.

"Oh, here you go with one of your acronyms. So what is an IBM?"

"Please allow me," Ivy said and turned to Sheena. "An IBM is an Ideal Black Man."

"Got it. So you all think Jason is my IBM?"

"I think he is," Miranda answered.

"So do I," Ivy agreed.

She looked at Jade who hadn't said a word. "What do you think?"

"Who am I to judge? I can't keep myself straight so I know I'm not going to try and tell you who's right for you."

"We're not judging here." Ivy placed a bottle of apple cider on the table and sat down. "We're just telling a tree by the fruit it bears. We all know that Sheena has been depressed since that man left here. We've all talked about it."

Miranda agreed. "She's right. The light has dimmed in your eyes, girlfriend."

"So don't think of this as judging," Ivy said. "Think of it as an inspection. We are fruit inspectors."

"Yeah, girl," Miranda continued. "I know an apple when I see it and I know it from a pear."

"Look... we all know a rotten apple when we see one." Ivy added.

Jade giggled. "Well, since you put it that way, come to think of it, you've been acting crazy ever since you told us about that argument you and him had at your office a few weeks before he left."

"Yeah, that's the right word. Just like Beyonce say in that song "Crazy In Love." Ivy commented.

"So tell us what's your dilemma, Sheena? Why'd you push him out of your life? 'Cause from what we've observed you are *crazy* in love with him." Miranda leaned back in her chair.

Sheena was silent and the silence stretched out for a minute or more before she blurted out, "I'm just not interested in Jason... romantically. We're friends. I like being around him. Being with him was like hanging out with one of you."

"Jason's not like one of us," Jade commented.

Miranda high-fived Jade. "Far from it. I may be saved, but I have eyes and that man is fine."

"I'm not interested in him that way. Not him or any other man."

Jade stopped filling her bowl with fruit and looked at Sheena inquiringly, remembering their conversation about Josephine.

"Jason and I were friends, that's all. Nothing more! I'm not interested in him in any other way," Sheena snapped, her eyes flashing.

"Well, once you get over Jason, there'll be someone else. But I tell you what, it better be soon, 'cause none of us is getting any younger!"

Sheena shook her head looking at Miranda. "Young or old, I'm not interested in any man."

Jade dropped the bowl on the table, startling everyone. "So who are you interested in?" She wasn't looking at the fruit; she was looking at Sheena.

Sheena thought about the question for a moment. "I'm not interested in anyone."

"When's the last time you talked to Josephine?"

"Yesterday. Why?"

"Why are you still talking to her? I thought we agreed that you didn't need to be around her."

Miranda and Ivy sat looking between the two other women as the verbal dueling began. This wasn't unusual between Jade and Sheena. There weren't many times all of them could come together and the two friends didn't debate about something.

Miranda adjusted her seat for the entertainment to come. "Here we go. I need some popcorn."

"I work with the woman, Jade. What am I supposed to do?"

"You're supposed to stay away from her. You know she's after you."

Miranda gasped. "After her?"

"Well, I don't want her. And even if I did, I told you, I'd never act on it."

Ivy almost choked on a slice of fruit.

Jade pressed on. "You and I already had this conversation the other day. You told me you were going to stay away from her. She's gay and you don't have any business hanging around her."

"I'm not hanging around her. I work with her."

"So what do you mean when you say you're not interested in any man?"

"'Cause I'm not. But I do feel more comfortable around women than I do men."

Both Ivy and Miranda's mouths were agape; they were clearly astonished by the conversation.

Jade ignored them. "So what are you saying, Sheena?"

"Look, I don't have control over Josephine. I don't have control over what she is or isn't. I only have control over me. I know that God made Adam and Eve. But I can't help how I feel. I'm more comfortable with women than I am with men."

Miranda stood up from her chair abruptly. "That's it." She pointed at Sheena. "We're taking you to the church and casting that demon out of you before he gets rooted!"

Ivy's mouth was open. She turned to Sheena. "I don't want to put words in your mouth so I want to be sure I understand you right. Josephine is into women?"

"Yes."

"And so you're saying that you're more into …" Ivy paused. "What *are* you saying, Sheena?"

"I'm saying that in all likelihood, I'll die an old maid. I don't want a man and I'm not interested in getting with a man. That's all, end of conversation."

Ivy lifted her head. "No, it's not the end of the conversation."

"Damn right it's not." Jade spat out.

"What guy have I ever dated more than twice? I'll answer that one for you: none. Tell me why I'm more comfortable around women than men. Just tell me."

Ivy tried to be calm when she answered. "It's because of your looks, Sheena. Your looks attract men. You have a sex appeal about you that's just natural. We know for a fact that you're oblivious to it."

"I don't wear make-up. I don't try to wear clothing that makes me stand out."

"That's my point. You can't even downplay your looks. It's natural. Men lust after you and you've been dealing with it a long time."

"Since puberty," Miranda tossed out and sat down.

"They're dogs. All of them are dogs. I hate how they look at me. It's sickening."

"That's not the way you feel about Jason. You don't think he's sickening." Ivy took both of Sheena's hands. "Sheena, honey, you're in love with Jason. That's why you're not interested in other guys, and that's the only reason why. You're comfortable around him. He looks at you with admiration and not lust. He respects you.

"Josephine is just…"

"A trick of the enemy." Miranda completed. "Satan is busy. His aim is to kill, steal and destroy. He's preying on you because you're weak right now. He knows you're hurt over your relationship with Jason."

Ivy shook her head. "You've always kept your guard up with men. Especially ones you don't know. Always!"

Miranda continued. "They're constantly gawking at you. You've always tried your best to act like it doesn't bother you, but we all know it does. So we just played if off like you do."

Jade placed her hand on Sheena's shoulder. "Don't allow Satan to use that woman and what she says to get to you. Don't let the devil make you think you're something that you're not."

"I would never act on it, no matter what. But, that's doesn't mean I can't be honest about how I feel." Sheena stood up.

"You let her get to you," Jade said accusingly.

"No, Satan got to her," Ivy corrected her.

"Look, I told you all I'd never act on it. Never! I'm a born-again believer. A Christian in my heart, and through every fiber of my being. So what I feel just doesn't matter."

Miranda asked, gently, "So is that why you and Jason aren't speaking anymore? All because you're confused?"

Sheena walked toward the family room and all the others followed behind her. "I'm not confused."

Ivy rephrased Miranda's question. "We're talking to you, Sheena. Is that the reason why you and Jason broke up your friendship?"

Sheena picked up her coat from the chair, blew out a sigh and said, "Jason's a Muslim."

"What?" Miranda exclaimed in surprise.

"You heard me right. He's a Muslim." Sheena put on her coat. "So is his entire family."

Ivy was dumbfounded. "But how can that be? He's even gone to church with us."

"Yes, only because I went to the temple with him."

"Why didn't you tell us?" Miranda asked.

"Because I didn't want any flack from any of you. Anyway, I went because I was curious. After going I knew that all we could be was friends. But we started spending more and more time together and naturally everyone expected us to take it to the next level. But I'm not changing gods for Jason or anybody." Sheena moved toward the front door. "And I'm not engaging in any lesbian relationships, offending God and myself, no matter how I feel." She turned to look at each of her friends as she stood in the entryway. "For God I'll live and for God I'll die."

Miranda moved in front of the door. "So, this woman … what's her name again?"

"Josephine," Jade supplied.

"This Josephine wanted to get with you … I mean like … lovers?"

Sheena said, coldly, "She never said anything to me like that. She never even approached me in that way."

"But Jade said the woman wants you … and you did mean sexually, didn't you?"

"That's exactly what I meant."

"The woman never came off to me that way." Sheena was becoming frustrated. She turned to Jade. "You know, if you want to tell a story you need to tell it correctly. This is how rumors start."

"So the girl didn't hit on you?" Jade asked aggressively.

"No. She only admitted to being gay, that's all. What she said was, and I quote, *they always find out about us. Even if we deny it, what's in us comes out.*"

"Come on, Sheena. You're an intelligent woman. She was saying that you are like her."

"And I told her I wasn't."

Miranda glanced at Jade before pressing Sheena even more. "So what about Jason?"

"What about him, Randi?"

"Did he want you to convert?"

"Oh, no, he never asked me to do that."

"Well, maybe *he's* willing to convert."

"He's been talking to José for two years now. All of you know how good José's ministry is when it comes to evangelizing lost souls to Christ." The women nodded. "Well, he hasn't been able to touch Jason."

"Sheena, you know everyone's not going to be saved. Some people are just tares. The Bible says let the wheat and the tares grow together and He would do the separating."

"I blame myself. I knew from the beginning. He never hid that fact about himself from me."

"You know, he never denied calling me to check on you. He even told me that living in Atlanta was like being in exile. No matter how many people he's around, it doesn't stop him from thinking of you."

Sheena clinched her teeth and blew out her frustration. "I hate that I ever met him!" she exclaimed.

"That's funny because he almost said the same thing about you. His exact quote was, *I wish I'd never met her*."

Jade nodded. "Call him, Sheena. You need to get everything out in the open. Communication is the key."

"A Christian and a Muslim? Please!" Miranda shook her head. "No way! I've read up on them. They believe there is no hope for us in Christianity, that it's a religion organized by *the enemies*."

Jade pushed her hands into her leather gloves. "That's the old Elijah Muhammad's teachings. Louis Farrakhan resurrected that old thinking after Elijah's son Wallace changed the name from the Nation of Islam to the American Muslim Mission. Since 1975 the movement has been accepted by orthodox Muslims as legitimately Islamic and within the fold of Islam."

"Oh, wow, I didn't know Elijah's son changed the old traditional American Black Muslim movement."

"Well, he did. Farrakhan rebelled against Wallace Muhammad. He left the group in 1977 and formed his own reorganized Nation of Islam. Jason's family doesn't follow Farrakhan."

"Well, if they aren't following Our Lord and Savior Jesus Christ, there's a problem from jump-street," Miranda responded.

All the women agreed.

"Look, I'll see you all Sunday. Jade, congratulations, and please let me know what I can do to help you put that quick wedding together."

"All right."

Sheena waved goodbye and escaped.

"Oh, we have to pray for homegirl."

Ivy turned to Miranda. "Sometimes we have to do more than pray." Ivy paused. "When Jason called you, did he leave his number?"

"No, but José has it. I'm sure I can get it from him."

"Good. I'm gonna have a little chat with Mr. Jackson."

☙☜

That night, Sheena sat at her computer reading her email. Still nothing from Jason; as a matter of fact, most of it was junk. She shut down the computer, still angry with herself for revealing her most intimate feelings with her friends. *Why did I do it?* Maybe because she wanted to discuss the whole sordid matter with her best friends just to find out what their thoughts were.

She looked at her telephone. Jade had said to call him. *Communication is the key.* She sat on the side of the bed, picked up the phone and started dialing his number. "Hello?" It was a woman's voice, and Sheena quickly put her finger over the hook to disconnect the call. A woman had answered Jason's phone! *He has women in every state*, she thought, feeling her stomach muscles tighten.

Sheena picked up the phone again and dialed another number. "Hello?"

She smiled, "Hi, Mommy."

"Hey, baby, how are you?"

"I'm surviving."

"I just talked to Jade's mother, she told me Jade and Darrell was getting married."

"Yes, I know. She brought us all together to gloat."

There was a snort of derision from the other end of the phone. "Is that how you feel about it?"

She twisted the telephone cord, feeling bad about saying it quite that way. "No, Mommy, I'm happy for her. She should have married Darrell years ago."

"Yes, she should have, but everything is in God's own time."

"Yes, I know you're right."

Her mother seemed to sense her mood and changed the subject. "So are you gearing up for this year's bowling tournament?"

"I'm not competing this year."

"Oh, you couldn't find a partner? Well, you should have asked Jason to fly in for..."

"No, Mother. Jason and I don't even speak."

"But I thought ..."

"Don't think, Mother." Her voice was cold.

"Must be pretty serious. You only call me mother when your temperament is in ruffles."

There was a long pause. "I just called to see how you were. Is Daddy home?"

"No, he's at the church with Reverend Jones."

"Oh, well, kiss him for me. I love you, Mommy."

Just before she hung up, her mother said softly, "Sheena."

"Yes?"

"This too shall pass. It's always the darkest before the light, you hear me?"

"Yes." She heard the beep on her phone signaling a call waiting. "I love you, Mommy. Let me catch this call."

"Okay, baby. 'Bye."

Sheena clicked to the other line. "Hello?"

"Why didn't you ask for me when you called?"

She smiled in spontaneous delight. "Well, hello to you, too, Jason."

"Hey, Sheen."

"I really didn't mean to hang up on your girlfriend. I hung up thinking I had the wrong number. But after I thought about it for a moment, I realized that it's typical of you to have at least one woman in every area code."

"Uh-huh. You're still funny, you know that? For your information, Ms. Smarty, Denise is my neighbor. Her husband locked her out of her apartment, not knowing she left without her keys."

"Oh, so she's hanging out with you until he returns?"

"No, she's using my phone to call her husband."

Sheena's smile widened. "Ooh, I see."

Jason debated whether he should tell her that Ivy had called and told him what had happened at her house just hours before. He decided against it. "So, what's up? Why'd you call me?"

"In all honesty?"

"Do you know any other way?"

"No."

"Then tell me. What's up?"

"I miss you, Jason." She paused and he did not interrupt her. "I called to apologize to you for everything that's happened between us. And … I just want us to … at the least be civil to one another."

"Sheen, when haven't I been civil to you? I respect you. And …"

"You won't talk to me, Jason. I haven't heard a word from you. Not even an email – I know 'cause I check everyday I've gotten nothing."

"Well, you hadn't contacted me until tonight."

"So, you'll only talk to me if I initiate it?"

He sounded frustrated. "You don't understand."

"Yes, I do. You're angry with me. You'd rather not talk to me or see me."

"I'm not angry with you. I'm angry with myself. I let my feelings for you get out of hand. I've never been in love before, Sheen. I just don't know how to handle this thing I feel for you. I thought getting away from you would help me get my feelings under control."

There was a long moment of silence.

"That's why I owe you an apology. I knew things between us were getting tense, and at first I honestly wanted to see where it would go. So, I just let it develop. I guess I led you on. So – I'm sorry for that. If I had known then what I know now, I would never have done that."

"What do you know now?"

She twisted the phone cord some more. "That I'll probably never marry or have children."

His voice was sharp. "Is that so? How did you come to that conclusion?"

"I'm not attracted to men, period. As a matter of fact, most of them disgust me."

A pause before he asked, "So what are you saying, Sheen?"

She sighed. "I'm saying that I'll die an old maid."

"What do you mean? Are you gay?"

"I don't engage in any sexual activity. So I'm not gay."

"Oh, yeah, that's right. Well, I'm sorry you feel that way. Personally, I think you'd make a wonderful wife and mother."

She sighed. He was trying, he really was, and she had to give him credit for that. "That's why I like talking to you, Jason. You understand me like no one else does. And I really want us to be friends again. So please accept my apology."

"We'll always be friends, Sheen."

She smiled, widely. "Good. So has anyone told you that Jade and Darrell are getting married?"

CHAPTER TWELVE

Jade turned to look out of her rearview mirror and caught a glimpse of Keith standing behind her car. *Oh, God, not today*, she prayed. She couldn't believe he had the nerve to show his face on campus. After the fiasco at the church, she thought she wouldn't ever hear from him again. Well, at least for a while, since he'd been arrested for violating the restraining order. She leaned on her horn, hoping to make him move. "Get away from my car, Keith!"

Keith leaned on the back of it. "You need to talk to me, Jade."

"I'm calling the police."

"So call them. I'm not afraid of the cops."

Darrell had told Jade if Keith contacted her again to call him. So instead of calling the police, she dialed Darrell's cell phone number.

"Hello?"

"Darrell."

He could hear the alarm in her voice immediately. "Hey, what's wrong?"

"I'm in the parking lot at the school and Keith is here. He's leaning on the back of my car and he won't get off."

"Give him the phone so I can talk to him."

Jade got out of the car. "Darrell wants to speak with you," she barked as she stretched her arm to give him her phone.

He looked at her suspiciously then took the phone. "Hello?"

"What do you want, Keith?"

"I want to talk. I need to get some things straight."

"Okay, let's meet Tuesday. My friend's office on Cooper Street. Six o'clock."

"Tuesday? Why not sooner?"

"Look, take it or leave it. Tuesday. And I promise you can say all you need to say. But right now, you're in violation of a restraining order."

Keith looked over at Jade. "That's only five days, I can do that."

"Good."

"Where did you say you want to meet?"

"My friend's office. It's on Cooper Street. Not far from where you are now." Darrell told him the address. "Now if you don't mind, let Jade go. I know you don't want to be arrested again, do you?"

"No." Keith gave the phone back to Jade. "I'll see you on Tuesday," he said as he walked away.

Jade slid back behind the wheel. "You made arrangements to meet with him?"

"We're going to have to deal with him, Jade. I just need to get my ducks in a row by Tuesday, that's all."

"Darrell, I don't know. He's really acting crazy."

"Don't worry about him. I'm going to handle it. Are you finished with classes for today?"

"Yes."

"Good, I'll meet you at City Hall. Then we're going shopping."

"Shopping for what?"

"I want to get you an engagement present for Sunday."

Jade was nonplussed. "What's happening on Sunday?"

"You're going to church with me. It's a big day: Pastor Jones is going to announce our upcoming nuptials!"

"Oh." She didn't know what else to say.

"See you in a few minutes!" His voice was cheerful.

"Wait," Jade said quickly. "Why do you want me to meet you at City Hall?"

"We need to pick up the marriage license, my love."

"Our blood tests are ready?"

"I have them in my possession. Can't get the license without 'em. Oh before I forget, the hospital asked if you would consider giving some blood. They said you have a rare type and it would be nice if you would donate some of it."

She put the car in reverse and waited until she had backed up successfully before speaking again. "I didn't know I have a rare blood type until my father went into the hospital. Just before his surgery I gave blood. So did Theashia. She has the same type I have.

"Well, I have a card for you. I told them I didn't think you'd mind giving. Right now you need to be getting to City Hall."

"Wow, you're moving really fast. I was thinking we could get married right after graduation. It will give me time to plan something nice."

"You know good and well I'm not waiting until May. Once we get the license we have thirty days. That's it, Jade, thirty days."

"Well, Ivy did it in less time. I guess I can, too." She pulled out of the parking lot and into the flow of traffic.

"You could be more enthusiastic about it than that."

Jade laughed. "I'm just … amazed, is all."

"I'll be excited enough for both of us. If I could, I'd shout my happiness for the whole world to hear."

"I must admit, you've shown more excitement than I've seen in a very long time."

"Come on, girl. Get a move on it."

"I'm only around the corner. I'll beat you there."

"I'm already here, baby. Park on the Market Street side of the building. I'm waiting for you."

℘ℭ

"Knock, knock!"

Sheena raised her head from the files she was reading to see Josephine standing in front of her desk. "Hey, you have that report for me?"

"Yeah." She handed Sheena a file folder. "If you give me another day I could be more thorough."

"No, that won't be necessary." She looked up. "But thanks anyway." She dropped her head back down to the file.

"It's 5:15. You gonna work late again tonight?"

Sheena nodded, not taking her eyes from the paper. Josephine didn't leave, and after a few minutes Sheena lifted her head again. "Is there something else you want?"

"I'd like to talk to you."

"Work-related?"

"No."

"Then we have nothing to talk about."

Still Josephine didn't leave. "If I offended you, I want to offer an apology."

Sheena never looked at her. "Accepted. Now if you'll excuse me, I need to get this done. Please close the door behind you."

Josephine turned and collided into someone coming in through the door. "Excuse me," she mumbled without looking to see who it was.

"No, problem. You all right?" It was Jason's voice.

Sheena tossed her files on the desk. "Jason!" She sprang from her chair, almost knocking him down a second time. She wrapped her arms around his neck and kissed his cheek. "Why didn't you tell me you were coming?"

"I wanted to surprise you." He looked over at Josephine. "You didn't hurt yourself did you?"

Josephine shook her head and left, and Jason pushed the door shut behind her.

Sheena was grinning from ear to ear. Jason looked at her for a moment. "Come on. Get your stuff and let's get out of here."

"Let me get my purse."

"I want an original Tarantini Panzarotti from Marlton Pike in East Camden."

"You gonna hang out with me like we use to?"

Jason smiled. "Videos, Monopoly, pigging out on junk food? That what you had in mind?"

"Why not? I can afford it."

"You sure can. Especially the junk food. How much weight have you lost?" He looked at her appraisingly.

Sheena found herself blushing. "I haven't lost any weight."

He nodded emphatically. "Yes, you have. When I put my arms around you, you almost got lost in my embrace."

She laughed. "It must be you. I think you've gained about forty pounds."

He took her hand and hugged her again. "I've missed you."

"I missed you, too."

ॐ✿ॐ

"If you don't like it, we can have it exchanged. You won't hurt my feelings." Darrell had purchased Jade's engagement ring earlier in the day. He gave the ring to her as soon as she got home from school. Now they were sitting in Darrell's car outside his parents' home.

"It's beautiful, Darrell." Jade held out her hand, admiring the ring on her finger. "But you didn't have to buy me a new wardrobe, too!"

"Three dresses and a pantsuit hardly constitute a whole new wardrobe."

Jade smiled. "Did I say thank you?"

Darrell lifted her hand to his lips and kissed it. "About three times already."

"Hmm …"

He didn't release her hand. "You don't mind eating dinner with my parents, do you?"

"No. But I would rather have changed clothes first."

He smiled and stroked the back of her hand with his thumb. "You're fine. My mother doesn't normally cook on Fridays and I think this is a last-minute thing. So don't expect much."

Jade sighed and looked at the front door.

His hand tightened around hers in concern. "What's wrong?"

She was silent for a moment. She turned to look at Darrell. "It's your father. He – makes me nervous."

"I'll be sure my father behaves himself. But it doesn't matter – we can leave when you're ready. Okay?" He squeezed her hand and then released it.

She nodded in agreement as she opened the car door.

"Isn't that your mother's car?" Darrell got out on his side and pointed at the gray Volvo parked across the street.

She glanced at the tag number. "Yeah, it is. I wonder –"

"Well," he broke in, "things can't get too bad, with your mom here. Come on, let's get it over with."

They walked to the front door. Darrell opened it and a shout of "Surprise!" engulfed Jade as he did. She turned to Darrell, "You set me up!"

"No way! I'm just as surprised as you are!"

"That's right, he didn't know a thing," Mrs. Parker confirmed as she hugged Jade. "Welcome, Jade. We're so happy for you."

Looking over Mrs. Parker's shoulder she saw her mother and sister. "Mama …" She hugged her next.

"Hey, big sis." Theashia kissed her cheek.

Jade put her hands over her face, laughing in embarrassment and amazement. Mr. Parker held Dee in his arms and she hugged them both. Jade had always been uncomfortable around him. But today felt different. The smile he gave her in return felt sincere. Dee was all giggles and she kissed her son's cheek.

They went into the living room together; it was full of enthusiastic guests. Looking around the room, Jade noticed people she hadn't yet met. She assumed they were co-workers and friends of Darrell. Everyone she cared about was there – well, everyone, that was, except Sheena. But she didn't have time to think about that; the noise was almost deafening as everyone offered their congratulations.

"Congratulations to both of you! You're years overdue, but better late than never," Mother Brown said as she handed Jade an envelope. "Now you know I didn't have a chance to get you a proper wedding shower gift, but your future mother-in-law told me money was always proper,' she said with a wide grin.

"Thank you, Mother Brown." Darrell and Jade spoke nearly in unison.

Mrs. Parker joined them. "Now listen up, everyone! This is what we're going to do." She walked toward the corner of the room and the crowd parted. That's when Jade and Darrell both noticed the undecorated artificial Christmas tree standing there in the corner. Mrs. Parker turned to them. "You're going to decorate this tree with money. 'Cause everyone here is supposed to bring money, even if it's only a dollar."

"That's right," Pastor Jones said. "Here's an envelope from me and my wife with our blessings for your upcoming special day." He handed Darrell the envelope.

"Thank you, Pastor, Mrs. Jones."

"My turn," Ivy announced. "Here's the envelope with a few dollars in it. But I've got something else for you, too. But you can't open it here. As a matter of fact, you can't open it until your honeymoon. It's for you and Darrell both."

Then Miranda chimed in. "Here's mo' money, mo' money... So congrats, girl. And … so it's known, I'm saying right here in front of everyone that the next baby you have is my godchild. So don't get it twisted, Ivy."

Everyone laughed and from that moment on the envelopes kept coming. It was simply a joyous occasion.

Soon after everyone gave their gifts, Jade remembered she hadn't seen Sheena. As she looked around the room she wondered if Sheena was upset with them.

Darrell noticed her mood. "What's wrong?"

She tilted her face up to him. "Sheena didn't come."

"I asked about her. Ivy said she's on her way, with Jason."

"*Jason?*"

Darrell nodded. "Yeah. It's my understanding that he flew in today and went straight to her office."

Jade smiled, hearing what she considered good news. "She hasn't been the same since he's been gone."

"Yeah, and I know that feeling, too!"

"Jason!" they heard Miranda screech. "Give me a hug, man!"

"Where's the happy couple?" Sheena asked. "There they are. Look at you! Glowing and everything."

Jade stood up. "No, you're the one that's glowing." She whispered in her friend's ear. "Did you two get back together?"

Sheena whispered back, "I don't know, but I'll give you the details later."

Jade stepped back and saw Jason shake Darrell's hand. "Now this celebration is complete. I'm so glad you came."

"You know I wouldn't have missed it unless I was in the hospital or the morgue."

Both women laughed.

Jade turned a little somber. "I wish my father could have been here."

"I'm not going to say to you he's here in spirit 'cause I know it would be nice to have him here, physically."

She looked toward her mother, "This is her first social event since he died." She looked at Sheena. "I see the sadness in her eyes. She hasn't been the same since he's been gone."

"Well, it may take a while. She was married to the man for how many years?"

"I think… what…thirty years."

"That's a long time. But she'll be all right. She's a strong woman. If she was going to lose it, it would have been months ago."

"I'm sure you're right."

⇚⇛

Mrs. Parker wouldn't allow Jade to do anything to help clean up after the gathering. Jade didn't worry about it too much because a few members of the church stayed to help clean up. She instructed her son to take his family home, so he did.

Dee didn't seem tired at all. Even after Jade gave him a bath, which usually made him go right to sleep, he was showing no signs of sleepiness.

"I want my daddy."

"Your father is going home. You need to go to sleep."

He shook his head and said, stoutly, "Gram said my daddy gonna stay at our house now."

Jade had to smile. "Yes, baby, that's true. But that's not happening tonight, okay?"

"Why not?" He was starting to pout.

She sighed. "Because it's not proper, okay?"

Definitely pouting. "*Why*, Mommy?"

"Go to sleep, Dee."

Darrell walked into the room and Dee looked at his father with tears in his eyes. "I want you to stay with us, Daddy!"

"I want to stay, too." Darrell wiped his son's eyes. "Tell you what, Dee. You go to sleep, and I promise I'll be here when you wake up, okay?"

Dee nodded his head vigorously.

Darrell came to the side of the bed and began to tuck the child in. Jade left and went into her bedroom.

Darrell came to Jade's doorway and stood there. Jade walked into the closet, removed her shoes and pushed her slippers onto her feet. "You know he gets up early, right?" She pulled her robe from the hanger and moved toward the bathroom.

"Yeah, I know. I'm staying here tonight."

Jade stopped moving. "What did you just say?"

"I'm staying here tonight."

Jade came into the bedroom and stared at him. "*Not* a good idea."

"Why not?"

"Darrell, don't be ridiculous. You know perfectly well why not." Jade walked across the room and removed a pair of pajamas from the dresser drawer. "Come on. It's late. I really don't feel like debating tonight, okay?" She started to the bathroom and stopped. "Temptation is sometimes stronger than will. Don't give it any help to defeat us, especially since we're so close to the end of this race."

"You're right. I'll go home."

Jade smiled. "Good." She walked into the bathroom and started the shower.

"Your mother wants to talk to both of us."

She adjusted the water then walked into the bedroom. "I noticed you two where talking a long time. Did you tell her you made arrangements to talk to Keith?"

"I sure did."

"Is she worried about it?"

"Maybe, just a little."

Jade stared at Darrell. "Well, to be honest I'm a little worried too."

"Don't be. Jason and Marshall are working on this for us."

"I really screwed up didn't I?"

Darrell smiled. "Don't do that."

Jade didn't pretend she didn't know what he was talking about. "Okay, I won't."

"Maybe we can have dinner with your mother tomorrow and she can talk with both of us then."

"Okay. I want her to be at ease and I know this thing with Keith has to be pulling on her emotional state. She was so gloomy this evening."

"She's going to be all right. I told her this too shall pass."

Jade stepped into the bathroom and closed the door. Leaning against the door, she shut her eyes tightly and silently prayed. "Father, you know my mother far better than me. She's a good woman with a huge heart. Give her the peace that passes all understanding. Bring joy back into her heart. Deliver all of us from evil... You are our strength and you are our redeemer. In Jesus' name I pray, Amen."

When Jade emerged from the bathroom thirty minutes later, she looked out her window and saw that Darrell's car was gone.

CHAPTER THIRTEEN

Sheena woke up the next morning feeling more rested then she'd felt in months. She smiled to herself, knowing that she'd slept straight through the night without even going to the bathroom. She hadn't done that in a long time, either.

Remembering she was supposed to have breakfast with her mother, Sheena called and cancelled the date; fortunately, her mother didn't ask for an explanation.

Sheena showered, washed and blow-dried her hair. She flat-ironed it, allowing her tresses to hang. It was rare that she straightened her naturally curly hair, but she had done it without even realizing she did so because Jason liked it that way.

When she entered the living room, the apartment was quiet. She assumed Jason was still sleeping. Her two-bedroom apartment had two complete bedroom suites, so Jason had plenty of privacy. Sheena made her way into the kitchen and smiled, remembering her mother's comment about paying penthouse prices for an apartment she rarely stayed in to enjoy.

"Well," she thought out loud, "I guess this is a good time to try out some of those cooking gadgets." Sheena had been attempting to learn the finer points of cooking for the last few months. Cooking was one skill at which she just was not a natural. Knowing how much Jason liked coffee, she poured out the remnants of what he'd brewed the night before and made a fresh pot. After that she pulled out a skillet to fry some turkey bacon, opened the freezer and took out the microwave pancakes, and thought about trying to make some from scratch, but decided against it. She was at the stove laying turkey bacon in the pan when Jason came into the kitchen.

"Good morning, sleepyhead!"

Without replying, he scratched his head and asked, "What do you think you're doing?"

"I'm cooking."

He chuckled. "Cooking? When did you learn to do that?"

Placing her hand on her hip she turned to him. "Oh, don't be funny." Both of them laughed: her lack of cooking skills was legendary. "Did you sleep well?"

"I slept just fine, thank you. I'm gonna get out of here and out of your way. Is my coat in the closet?"

"Oh, no, you don't. I know you don't think I'm eating all this bacon and these eggs and pancakes by myself."

"Eggs!" He raised his eyebrows in comic disbelief, "Is that what that is?"

She had to laugh. They did look a little deformed. "Okay, you know exactly what that is."

Jason leaned on the counter. "Get dressed. I'll take you out to breakfast."

"No, thank you, I'm eating this."

"Okay, if you end up with stomach pain and get sick, I'm not taking you to the hospital," he said, trying to keep a straight face.

"If I do end up needing medical treatment, you'll take me."

"No, I won't.

"Oh, yes you will."

"No, I won't," he countered.

"Let me eat this and get sick, then we'll see."

"What makes you so sure I wouldn't let you suffer in agony?"

She thought about it only a second before saying instinctively, "Cause you love me."

The sizzling of the bacon frying suddenly sounded very loud in the still room, and the silence stretched out between them. Jason moved and stood directly behind her. Sheena felt the atmosphere shift because of those four words. *Cause you love me. Why did I say that?* She wondered.

"If you know that, then why are we persecuting ourselves?" he asked, his lips so close to her ear that his breath was a soft caress.

She had no answer. She shrugged her shoulders.

A long moment passed before he put his arms around her waist. "You're right. I do love you. With my whole heart, mind, and soul. You love me, too. I know you do. It showed when you greeted me in your office yesterday."

She didn't deny it. How could she? She closed her eyes tightly. Ivy had to be right. She only felt like this when she was with Jason. No one else made her weak in the knees. Nobody made her feel like she had butterflies in her stomach. This only happened with Jason.

He reached over and turned off the fire under the skillet.

She turned to face him. "It's no secret that I love you."

His voice tightened. "Then tell me why you're here, and I'm not?"

She laid her head on his chest. "I don't know."

Jason turned while holding her. He lifted her, placing her on the counter and sandwiching his body between her legs.

She should have moved, but she didn't. She couldn't. And why should she? She liked being this close to him.

He wrapped his arms around her. Getting her as close to him as he possibly could, he felt her trembling. "Are you cold?"

"No." Her voice was just above a whisper.

"Are you afraid of me?"

"No. I'm not scared of you."

"Then why are you shivering?"

Sheena never realized she was until he asked. "I don't know." Her voice quivered too.

He placed his forehead against hers. "Maybe you're nervous." Then he kissed her. It was brief. Soft. Sweet.

Her swift intake of breath indicated to him that she enjoyed it. She licked her lips.

He rubbed her arms. "I feel goosebumps."

Sheena looked into his eyes and asked breathlessly, "Will you kiss me again?"

He answered by dropping his head and kissing her. He smiled when he lifted his head and saw her take her bottom lip into her mouth.

Oh, what a feeling, she thought. She wanted more.

Jason nuzzled her neck. "I don't think there should be any more questions about your sexuality."

Sheena stiffened. "Jade talked to you?"

"No," he said, still holding her.

"Ivy?"

"Ivy."

"So that's why you're here?" Some coldness had crept into her voice.

"No, I'm here because after I talked to you, I realized I needed to see you. I realized how much I missed you."

Her eyes filled with tears. "I miss you."

He kissed her again, lifted his head and smiled. "Have you been with anyone else this way?"

She shook her head, "No, never."

"Not even in college?"

She shook her head again. "I didn't date in college."

He remembered what she'd told him some years ago. "Oh, yeah, that's right. You didn't have time to date. You were too busy trying to stay focused on your studies." He traced her nose with his index finger. He kissed her again.

She surprised him by parting her lips and deepening the kiss. It seemed that just when he was about to immerse himself in the pleasure of it, she pulled away. She was going to say something, but he used the tips of his fingers to barely touch the surface of her face. He murmured, "I love you."

Oh God! It wasn't what he said, but the way he said it. She was losing control. This was too erotic. *Dangerously so* ... she thought. *Ooh* ...

Jason had never been this aroused before by mere touching. Only this woman could make him feel like this. He kissed her neck, over and over again.

"We ... have to ... stop ... Jason."

Instantly, he stopped and backed away from her. "Yeah, you're right. You've got me in a sweat."

Sheena swallowed hard. "Forgive me."

"There's nothing to forgive. But we're going to talk about this when things cool down, okay?"

Sheena nodded. "Help me off this counter."

After he put her on her feet, he moved away from her. "You get dressed. I'm taking you out to eat and I don't want to hear another word about it."

ౠగ్రஜ

When Jade opened her eyes the next morning, Darrell was sitting in the chair in the corner of the room watching her. She pulled the sheet up to her neck. "What are you doing here?"

"Didn't I promise my son I'd see him in the morning?"

"Then you should be sitting in *his* room."

"I like the scenery in here much better." He grinned appreciatively.

Jade smiled in response. "What time is it?"

"Eight-forty-five."

"Hmm," she said. "I'm surprised he's not up already."

"I'm not," he responded. "It was past eleven when he went to sleep."

"You're right." She looked around for her robe.

Darrell stood and picked up the robe that was hanging on the back of the chair. "Looking for this?" He handed it to her.

"Thanks. Now, if you'll leave …"

"That's okay: I'm going to go wake him up. See you in the kitchen."

By the time Jade made her way to the kitchen, Darrell was stirring cheese into a pot of grits. Dee was sitting at the table attempting to scramble eggs.

"Look, Mommy! I mix eggs!"

Jade kissed him on the forehead. "Yes, you are, and you are a very good helper, too."

Darrell opened the refrigerator door. "You need to go shopping. You don't have bacon or sausage … and where is the butter?"

"We don't eat a lot of pork, you know that." She walked over to the refrigerator, and leaning past him, pulled out a container. "We use margarine. Taste it, you won't believe it's not butter." She caught his expression. "What? Butter has too much fat. It clogs the arteries."

"That's why you bless it, Jade."

"We can also use good common sense, Darrell. The Lord surely expects that, too."

"Mommy, Daddy said I can have a baby brother."

Jade looked over at Darrell. "Oh, he did?"

Dee nodded happily.

Darrell took the bowl of eggs Dee had been stirring. "You want cheese and mushrooms in your eggs?"

Dee shook his head. "Just cheese, Daddy."

"I know you want just cheese. I was talking to your mother."

Jade sat down at the table. "Plain, thank you." She hadn't stopped staring at Darrell. "I guess you told Dee that because you want more children?"

"Of course I do. Two more, at least."

"I see," she said coldly. "I guess we should have talked about this before agreeing to get married."

"Jade, that's the purpose of marrying. Procreation."

Jade looked over at her son as Darrell put a plate of food in front of him. "You want milk or juice, honey?"

"Milk," he answered triumphantly.

Jade had vowed to never have another child. But at the time, she never thought she and Darrell would get back together.

Darrell put a plate in front of her and sat down at the table. "Let's pray. Father, bless the food and the hands that prepared it. Purify it from any dangerous substance so that it can be nourishment to our bodies. In Jesus' name we pray, amen."

"Amen, Daddy!"

Darrell smiled at his son then looked at Jade. She had picked up her fork but hadn't started to eat. "Something wrong with the food?"

"No. I just lost my appetite." She got up.

"Where you going?"

"I don't know," she said. "I'm not hungry."

"Sit down, Jade. Please." Jade glared at him. "*Please*."

She slid back down in the chair. She looked over at Dee eating his food, then at Darrell who was staring at her. "Talking about having another child bothers you that much?"

"Now is not the time, Darrell."

"I didn't mean now. But in a year or so …"

She shook her head. "I mean it's not the time to talk about it. I don't want to discuss it in front of our son."

"Why not?"

"I don't feel comfortable talking about this in front of a child." Jade got up again and left them in the kitchen eating. She could feel her heart thudding in her chest. She went into the family room and picked up the phone to call Ivy.

"Hey."

"Hey, Jade. I was about to call you!"

"Really? What's up?"

"Well, for one thing, I've made an appointment for a full day of beauty treatment at Cassandra's. Are you up for that?"

"It sounds good to me. I really, really need to get out of here."

"Well, the kids are hanging out with Bill today. So can you get to her shop by eleven?"

Jade looked at her watch. "I think I can do that."

"Great! We'll have fun." Ivy sounded delighted.

Jade hesitated. "He's hanging out with the kids, huh? You and Bill are getting mighty close, aren't you?"

"Don't start on that. Bill has been a very good friend to me since Ray's been gone."

"Uh-huh."

"I'm serious. If it weren't for Bill …"

"Jade!" It was Darrell. She looked across the room and saw him with his arms crossed over his chest. "Hang up the phone, and let's talk."

Ivy's voice was in her ear. "Earth to Jade …"

Jade turned her attention back to the telephone. "Hold that thought and we'll talk when I see you."

"Eleven, not eleven-thirty or twelve," Ivy said warningly. Jade was known for being late.

"I'll see you at eleven." She placed the phone back in its cradle.

Darrell held out his hand. "Come here, and let's sit down so we can talk."

Jade took his hand and allowed him to guide her to the sofa. Instead of sitting on the sofa next to her, he sat on the coffee table to face her. "Listen, baby. I didn't know that you didn't want to have any more children."

"I'm sorry I never said anything. But all of this happened so quickly."

"I've always wanted more than one child; you know that. I was an only child and I never liked it."

"Dee has a sister."

"No, Jade, Dee has an aunt." She started to disagree, but he had spoken the truth. "Children are a blessing from God."

"I agree. I just don't want to go through it again."

"What do you mean? Through the pregnancy?"

"Yes. It's horrible. I hated it both times. I don't want to go through it again."

He understood now. Darrell took both her hands in his. "Look at me." She raised her head to look at him. "You were alone. Both times." Darrell searched for the right words to soothe her. But deep in his soul, he knew that he would have been there for her if he had known about Dee. "I promise you, I'll be here for you every step of the way. I'll go to doctor's visits with you. I'll rub your back when it hurts and your feet when they're swollen." He got a smile from her. He smiled back. "I won't leave you alone unless God takes me home. I promise you."

"How many more?" she asked softly.

"Let's agree on one. After that we'll see what happens." She dropped her head and he followed by lowering his head to keep eye contact with her. "Okay?"

She nodded.

"I'm taking Dee to the arcade and then we're going for pizza. You want to go?"

"I just told Ivy I'd meet her at the salon."

He reached into his pocket and pulled out his wallet, handing her three hundred-dollar bills. "Here you go, baby. Enjoy."

"I don't need them, Darrell, but thanks. Pastor Owens gave me a three-hundred-dollar bonus."

"You sure?" The doorbell rang.

"Positive."

"You expecting anyone?"

"No. But I'll get it. The way things are going, it's probably Keith Strickland."

Darrell moved quickly. "Then I'll get it."

Jade smiled and headed toward the kitchen to check on Dee. She was clearing the table when Darrell walked into the kitchen with her mother. Dee saw the older woman first. "Nana!" The child sprang from his chair to greet his grandmother with a hug.

"Hello, my love." She lifted him and hugged him tightly, giving him kisses all over his face.

"Nana, my daddy gonna live with me and Mommy in our house."

She smiled. "I know, and I can tell you're very excited about that."

Dee bobbed his head up and down. "I'm gonna get a baby brother too."

"Dee!" Jade gasped.

Nora chuckled. "Well, that's going to be something, isn't it?" Again Dee nodded his head.

"Oh, it's okay. He can tell Nana anything he wants. Right, my sweetheart?" She cuddled her grandson close to her.

Dee nodded his head.

"Mama, why didn't you tell me you was coming over this morning? We could have had breakfast together."

She turned to Jade. "I didn't know I was coming. I … well, I've been praying … actually I been questioning God about what to do. When … to do it."

Jade looked at her mother suspiciously. "Mama, what's wrong? You're not sick or anything like that, are you?"

"No, I'm fine. I just had a physical last month. I'm the picture of health."

"Well, that's good to hear." She wasn't convinced.

"It's just that your daddy left me in such a pickle."

Here it is again, Jade thought. That same statement, *He left me in a pickle*. "Mama, what's wrong?"

"Come on, Dee. You can watch cartoons for a little while." Darrell picked Dee up and headed to the family room.

"Darrell!" Nora called.

"Yes, ma'am?"

"I want you here …"

He nodded. "I'll be right back. I'm just going to get him settled in the other room."

Jade could tell her mother was nervous. "Come on in, Mom. Let's sit down here in the kitchen. You want some coffee?"

"No, I had a whole pot already this morning." She pulled out a chair and sat down.

"Is something wrong with Theashia?"

"No, Theashia is fine. Let's just wait until Darrell gets back in here."

"Mama, if there's something you need to tell me, we don't need Darrell. You and I have always been able to talk."

"Yes, we have, haven't we?" Nora smiled as if at a memory.

Jade smiled. "Yes, even if we didn't agree."

Her mother paused before saying, "Yes, you're right," she sighed. "It's just that your father left me in such a pickle. He really should have done this himself. But he was right. The time just wasn't right."

"Mama, what are you talking about?"

She reached across the table and took Jade's hand. "I have to tell you some things, baby. Your father and I had only been married a little over ten years when we first met you. It was during that time I found out I would never be able to carry a child. That's when I stopped talking to God. I stopped going to church. I didn't want anything to do with a God who promised to give me the desires of my heart and then didn't deliver."

Darrell came into the room and sat next to Jade at the table.

"Then God sent us you. You said something to me one night that I'll never forget as long as I live."

Jade was baffled. "What, Mama?"

"You may not remember, because God used you to speak to my heart. You spoke with such wisdom."

"I'm sorry, Mama, I don't have a clue."

You came to me and your daddy one night. It was right after we found out about Theashia …"

"Can I talk to the two of you?"

Nora removed her eyeglasses and placed them on the nightstand. "Sure, come in." She patted the side of her bed.

Jade sat there. "I want to ask you … I mean… I want to know… if you believe in God?"

"What kind of question is that?"

Nora held up her hand to stop her husband. "I believe in God."

"Then why don't we go to church like everybody else?"

She sighed. "Because I really haven't had anything to say to God."

"Why?"

"Because I've been upset with God for a long time."

"Why?"

Nora paused, then looked over to her husband. Even he wanted to hear the answer to that question. "God promised to give me the desires of my heart and he never delivered."

"What was your desire?"

"To have a child of my own."

Jade paused, thinking about the answer for a moment. "If you had children of your own, you probably wouldn't have taken me in. You probably wouldn't have entered into the foster care program."

"I don't know that."

"I know that. You would have been fulfilled if you had children of your own. You wouldn't have been in the program to rescue me."

Nora thought for a moment, then answered. "That's possible."

Her husband stirred next to her. "She's right, Nora. We only entered the program because we couldn't adopt. So let's be honest with the girl."

"What's your point, Jade?"

"You're angry with God because he needed you to be in a position to help me. God is giving you the desire of your heart, it's just not coming from your own body. Does it matter how *God blessed you as long as He's blessing you?"*

Nora dropped her head.

"Answer her, baby." Her husband took her hand and gave it a quick squeeze.

Nora looked to her husband. "No, it shouldn't matter."

"I know you wanted what you wanted when you wanted it. But the fact of the matter is, I needed you more. The baby I'm carrying needs you now."

Nora wiped a tear from her eye and nodded as she looked at Jade.

Jade began twisting the birthstone ring on her finger her parents had given her for Christmas. "I know I'm only fifteen. By the time I have this baby, I'll be sixteen and I still won't be able to care for it. I need to finish school and I wanna go to college. But I won't give my baby up to just anybody, to just strangers."

"*Baby... Keith and his parents already signed. They don't want anything to do with this child. They've given up all rights. If Jade wants us the take the child, let's do it.*"

"*I don't know, Alan.*"

"*Why can't we adopt this baby?*"

"*Cause it will be a problem.*"

Jade shook her head. "*How? Not by me. I'll be a big sister, that's all. I can be a part of this child's life always.*"

"*Jade... baby... it's not that simple.*"

"*I heard the voice of God. You might not be speakin' to Him, but I heard Him loud and clear. I will not give my baby to strangers. If you don't want it, then I'll...*"

Nora grabbed Jade. "*No, it's not that I don't want the baby. I just know how cruel people can be. If we keep the child every tongue in this community will be wagging and...*"

"*We'll move!*" *Alan was sharp.*

"*What?*" *Nora said, surprise in her voice.*

"*We'll move to another state. Somewhere people don't know us.*" *Alan moved closer to Nora. He knew in his heart that this would be a great opportunity for his wife.* "*It will give Jade a chance to start over and it will protect the child from wagging tongues.*"

The room was silent. Nora couldn't believe her husband had said that. She saw the smile that crossed Jade's face.

"*Thank you, Daddy.*"

He smiled and nodded. "*No, thank you baby. Your mother always wanted a baby of her own. That was something I could never give her.*" *He smiled at Jade again.* "*So, it's settled. I'll call that attorney tomorrow and tell him what Jade wants. He's already familiar with the case so I think it can be done rather quickly.*"

"So I'm going to be a big sister, right, Daddy?"
"Right. You're going to be a wonderful big sister."

"You remember that conversation?"

"Vaguely."

"Well, God used you that day. After that He and I got on speaking terms again."

Jade smiled. "Imagine that, God using me. But, Mama, that's a good thing. I mean, why would you need Darrell to tell me that unless …"

Darrell placed his hand on Jade's. "Let her finish, baby."

The room was silent for a moment. An unsettled feeling came over Jade. Her mother stood up and walked over to the sink. "When your father had his operation, we were all asked to give blood." She took a glass from the cabinet and filled it with orange juice. "Even Theashia wanted to give." She returned to her seat at the table. "Your father had a rare type. You and Theashia have that same rare blood type."

"I was told something about Duffy?"

"Yeah, that's right. Anyway, you were a perfect match and just before the surgery your father asked the doctor to do DNA testing on all three of you." Nora took a sip from her glass. "The test came back 99.7% that my husband is your father."

Jade gasped and put her hand over her mouth.

"We didn't know, Jade. God knows I didn't know a thing. Your father had me to research your family background. He was interested particularly in your mother, and when I told him your mother's name was Maxine Smith, he didn't know who she was. I remember telling him that he'd been with so many women that he'd forgotten about this one. But your father was adamant when he said he remembered every single woman he'd ever been with – he said his list was very short. He said he'd never known anyone named Maxine Smith. He asked me to do a little more research. I didn't do it right away. He had his surgery and we mostly stayed at the hospital – you remember?"

Jade was still in shock and simply shook her head.

After your father was well enough, he wanted to know what I found. Well, the only thing I found was at the library. It was about a female being found in an abandoned house and the body being identified as that of Maxine Vernee Smith. "You father knew immediately who she was, from the name Vernee. He said he never knew her first name was Maxine.

"I only knew her as Max," Jade said.

"Well, I wanted to know about their relationship. But he told me that they'd only dated twice and he hardly knew her. He said he didn't remember what she looked like. But he remembered her name, because it was unusual. He said he found out that she …" Nora stopped mid-sentence, lowered her head and became silent.

"Mama, it's all right." Jade could see that she was choked up. There was nothing that her mother could tell her about Max that would shock her. But knowing that her father had anything to do with Max – that did shock her. Her father had been a man of high moral standards. It was shocking to her that he and Max would even run in the same circles.

"Your father left me in a pickle."

Jade gave a weak smile. Now she understood why she often stated that. "Yeah, I see that. He *did* leave you in a pickle."

Nora looked directly into Jade's eyes. "I loved him, Jade. I wasn't going to persecute him for something he'd done years before I'd met him."

"You're right, Mama. My grandmother told me Max never told her anything about my father. I assumed she didn't know who he was." Jade blew out a sigh. "I know that she was a promiscuous woman."

"Well, I knew your father hasn't always been the man we know and love. But he told me when you learn better, you do better."

"Yes, he told me that many times."

"Your father didn't know, Jade. He never knew he'd fathered you. If he had known … You'd never have been in foster care. Period."

Jade didn't even have to think about that. "I know, Mama."

"I wanted to tell you about this as soon as I found out. But your father didn't. He told me that he knew he wasn't going to be here long. To tell you about him being your biological father … He said … Well… He just didn't want you to experience two deaths."

"I understand."

Jade had taken the news much better than her mother had expected. "You aren't angry with me?"

"How can I be angry with you? You've been … better than a mother. You've been my friend. I love you."

"What about your father?"

"Oh, Mama, how can I judge him? He only did what he thought was right." Jade smiled, thinking about the decisions she'd made in her own life. "I guess the apple really doesn't fall far from the tree."

Her mother chuckled. "I guess you're right about that."

Jade looked at Darrell. "So now I know who my father is."

Darrell smiled as he nodded. You're an only child just like me. Our families are too small so you and I have an obligation to expand it. Darrell stood and pulled Jade into his arms and whispered into her ear. "No less than two more."

Jade leaned back and smiled up at him.

CHAPTER FOURTEEN

Jade was only three minutes late but Ivy didn't let her get away with even that. "I swear, Jade, you can't be on time for anything."

"I left home on time. Can I help that they had a ten-car accident on route forty-two?" Jade joked.

"Liar," Ivy snapped.

"Stop fussing and give me a hug."

Cassandra interrupted them. "Hi, Jade. Long time no see, girl. I want a hug too."

Jade wrapped her arms around Cassandra. "It has been a while, Cassandra. Don't think I haven't come because I didn't need a good hairdo!"

Cassandra examined Jade's hair. "You know I'm going to have to give you a hot oil treatment."

"Do what you have to. Just be sure to keep my bill two-hundred or less."

"Actually, today is your lucky day. All today's beauty has been paid by Ivy. Let me get you two started before the others get here."

"Miranda's coming?"

"Yeah, and so is Sheena," Ivy answered.

"You've talked to Sheena today?"

"Yeah, and she said she'll be a little late. Jason's staying with her."

"Really ..."

Ivy nodded. "Uh-huh. He's staying with her for the whole weekend."

"Oh, I see. He decided to pay her a visit after you called him."

"Something like that." Ivy flashed a quick smile.

Jade glanced around and lowered her voice. "Did he talk to her about what ... well, you know ..."

Yeah, he said he did. He said she's straight now. But when he got to her office on Friday, Josephine was there."

Jade shook her head. "She still don't have enough sense to stay away from that girl."

"Jason said she was putting her out. He said he heard her tell Josephine that the only thing they had to talk about was work. Nothing else."

"He eavesdropped?" Jade's eyes widened.

Ivy nodded. "I don't think it was intentional."

Jade shook her head and ducked into the bathroom, and Ivy and Cassandra exchanged wry glances. Cassandra seemed to be about to say something, but instead began writing a note in her daybook.

"Hello, hello, hello, to everyone." Miranda floated into the room.

Ivy looked at her and her eyes widened. Miranda looked absolutely radiant. "What happened to you? You hit the million-dollar lottery?"

Miranda giggled. "No ... something much better! I just learned that I'm up for a promotion. An important one."

Ivy smiled "That's great, Randi! You got the news yesterday?"

"Yeah and I've been floating on air ever since. I don't think I've felt this good since the day I met Kyle."

"You just met Kyle."

Miranda giggled. "Don't you be mad 'cause God's light is shining on me."

"No, I'm happy for you, Randi. When will you know if you got it?"

"By the end of the month. Where is Jade, and how come we're the only ones here? Cassandra, you're usually crowded on a Saturday."

She looked up from the daybook. "Actually, I was closed today. Ivy called me and asked me to open the shop for a special occasion."

"What special occasion?"

"Jade's getting..."

Ivy cut Cassandra off. "Jade's engagement announcement's tomorrow. It's going to be done during church service and she has to look her best."

Jade came out of the restroom. "Ivy, you didn't have to get Cassandra to open the shop for that."

Cassandra laughed. "Ooh, I don't mind. Ivy is being very generous to me and my staff. The only one who couldn't come was Brittney."

Miranda pretended to pout. "Well, who's gonna wash my hair since Brittney's not here? You know she has the magic hands."

"Renée. Believe me, you'll be happy with her."

›‹›‹

Cassandra was setting Ivy's hair. Miranda and Jade were getting their hair washed in another room, so they were alone. Cassandra whispered to Ivy, "Didn't you tell me you wanted the shop opened because Jade was getting married?"

"Yeah, but she doesn't know it yet."

"How in the world is someone going to get married and not know it?" She shook her head, clucking her tongue.

Ivy handed her a paper to put on the next curler. "Darrell called my father last night and told him that he wanted him to do it after Sunday's church service. My father called me this morning and told me to get the social hall ready and have the church mothers prepare the food. He said Jade already agreed to have the ceremony quickly. She just doesn't know it's tomorrow."

Cassandra met her eyes in the mirror. "Suppose she says no?"

"Then we'll have an engagement dinner. In any event, make sure you're in church tomorrow."

"Girl, I wouldn't miss this for the world!"

Sheena arrived just as Ivy was about to get under the dryer the other girls were getting their hair wrapped. "Hello, everyone!"

Miranda answered. "Hey, Sheena. What took you so long?"

"Well, I started to cook, but Jason didn't want it. So…"

All the girls started to snicker but Ivy doubled over in laughter. "You cook. Please… That man ain't crazy… he knows that's not one of your skills."

Sheena rolled her eyes at Ivy. "Anyway, we went to Elgin's Diner and got caught up in conversation so that's why I'm late." Sheena looked around the shop. "Where's everyone? You're never deserted on a Saturday, Cassandra."

The Cassandra chuckled. "I'm just catering to Ivy and her best friends today."

"The whole shop for the four of us?"

"Just for you."

"Wow, I feel special!" Sheena grinned. "Thanks, Ivy."

All the women were sitting in chairs having pedicures when Jade said, "I found out who my father is."

All the women were silent and Jade told them what her mother had told her earlier.

"Oh my God. What is the likelihood of the man that raised you ending up really being your father... like a billion to one?" Ivy asked.

"More like a zillion to none," Jade answered.

"You seem calm about it?" Miranda stated.

"I love them both. He loved me even when he didn't know I was his biological child. I think that was more important to me than anything."

"He probably loved you more when he found out." Sheena said.

"I don't know how that could be. He loved me unconditionally regardless."

Miranda shook her head. "Yeah, you're right about that. I couldn't tell by either of them that you were adopted or wasn't blood."

"Knowing this only made me love them more."

Ivy shook her head. "I can understand that."

Miranda and Sheena agreed.

Jade became misty after thinking about her parents. Lately she had been showing a lot of emotions that she normally held at bay or simply didn't feel at all. But this whole week had been emotional. Jade felt things she never felt before. But mostly she felt loved. "Where did Bill take the kids?" Jade put her hand up to her eyes.

"I think they went to the movies. He's probably going to take them to get something to eat, too"

Miranda shook her head. "He hangs around your house like he lives there."

"He's not there that much." Ivy was feeling defensive.

Miranda raised her eyebrows. "Maybe not to you, but I say that when a man starts answering your telephone, he's no longer just a friend of your dead husband."

"When have you called my house and Bill answered my phone?"

"Yesterday." She sounded triumphant.

Ivy dismissed it with a shrug. "That's because my hands were in dough."

Jade exchanged smiles with Miranda. "Oh, so he watches you cook now?"

"Stop it, Jade! Bill is just a good friend. He's been a father figure for the kids, especially the boys. They need someone like him around. I can't teach them to be men."

Sheena cleared her throat. "Leave her alone, girls."

Jade snapped, "I'm just trying to get the girl out of the clouds. You've never dated anyone but Ray, so I'm just trying to get you in touch with what's going on. The man can't stay away from you."

"Now, all of you know, Bill helped me get the house built and he took care of all my business after Ray passed away. Naturally, I would be close to the man. He's been more than a friend."

"That's my point," said Jade.

"What is your point?"

"The key words here are *more than a friend*."

Ivy shook her head. "You know what? I'm not going to entertain you." She turned to Sheena. "So let's change the topic. You and Jason having breakfast together sounds good. You aren't confused anymore, are you?"

Sheena didn't dare pretend she didn't know what Ivy was talking about. "Let me get something straight. I was never confused. So don't get it twisted. Besides… Jason told me you called him."

"So? I'd call him again, too."

"I know you would. Thank you, Mother Ivy." Sheena flashed her a smile.

Ivy rolled her eyes. "Had me all worried about you. Girl, I was ready to take you to the altar and have that demon prayed out of you."

Miranda laughed. "She really did. She wanted me and Jade to agree to take you to the altar, even if you were kicking and screaming."

Sheena looked over at Jade. "Are they serious?"

"As brain cancer."

Ivy wasn't finished making the rounds of her friends' problems. "So when are you getting married?" she asked Jade.

"Probably at the end of the month, unless Darrell wants it sooner."

"So it's really going to happen this time?" There was nothing but idle curiosity in her voice, as if she didn't know anything about what was happening.

"What choice do I have? I love the man to distraction, I already have his son and I'm living in his house."

"You got a point," Miranda conceded.

Ivy said, "So if Darrell said let's do it tomorrow, you would?"

Without thinking about it Jade answered, "Yeah, I would. Every time we're together, I feel drawn by temptation. Marriage is the only thing that can make us free."

"Well, you need to get the license and blood work."

She laughed "Already done! We did it all on Thursday. Darrell already gave the license to Pastor Jones."

"Can't call Darrell slow-footed," observed Sheena, and they all laughed.

Jade said, "I told Darrell that Pastor's study would be fine. But he rather have it in the church sanctuary, even if it's just Pastor Jones, him and me"

"I don't blame Darrell. You need to have your ceremony in a place of holiness. When I get married, I'm going to have a *huge* wedding." Miranda's eyes were alight with merriment.

Jade cut in. "You think that's going to be Kyle? And, speaking of Kyle, why haven't we met him yet?"

"He's coming to church with me tomorrow. So all of you can meet him then."

"Is it getting serious, Randi?" Ivy's eyes were wide.

"Look, I don't know what serious is. Me dating the same guy more than twice is serious to me. Do you know of anyone I've dated more than once since my high school prom date?"

Ivy laughed. "Come to think of it, nobody."

"I rest my case."

Jade said, in a small scared voice, "Darrell's meeting Keith next week."

"I wouldn't give him the time of day," Miranda said huffily.

"No,' Ivy said. "I think it's a good idea. Get everything out of the way. Them talking man to man is a good thing."

Sheena agreed. "I think she's right. Tell Darrell to call Marshall, he's an expert when it comes to family law."

Cassandra appeared in the doorway. "Come on, Jade. Now that your feet are done, let me start on your nails."

"I don't need my nails done."

Cassandra put her hand on her hip. "I beg to differ. Get your behind out of that chair and move it to the manicure section. Now! Please."

"Cassandra, where's the sparkling apple cider?"

"I have it on chill. It should be ready by the time I get you all in the main styling area."

CHAPTER FIFTEEN

Darrell and Jade arrived at the church around nine forty-five that Sunday morning. Mrs. Jones immediately escorted them to the pastor's study. After making small talk about how nice the surprise wedding shower had been, Pastor Jones turned serious.

"I wanted to speak to the two of you together because I never agree to announce a marriage that I'll be conducting without counseling with the couple." Pastor Jones had known Darrell all his life. His parents had been faithful members of Cathedral, joining the congregation as children under his father's reign; and Jade had been his daughter's friend since the day her family moved into the neighborhood. "I'm going to ask you some questions that I ask all couples."

He stared at both of them for a moment. "All right. What I want to know, first, is are you sure you want to marry and spend the rest of your lives together?"

Darrell spoke first, "I'm positive, Pastor. I've desired this woman from the day I met her."

Jade looked the pastor straight in the eyes and said, "There's nobody I'd rather be with than Darrell."

The pastor nodded. "Darrell, you confessed to me that the temptation between the two of you is great."

"It is. I'm weak when it comes to her. I need to marry quickly."

"How quickly?"

"Pastor, anytime you can perform the ceremony!"

Pastor Jones looked at Jade. "What are your feelings, Jade."

"We've already waited a long time, Pastor. We should have married a long time ago. I think the quicker the better."

Pastor Jones sat back in his chair, clasped his hands together and twirled his thumbs. "So if I wanted to perform a ceremony for you at this very moment, neither of you have a problem with it?"

Darrell looked at Jade. "I don't. Do you?"

Jade thought it was a rhetorical question, "No."

The pastor paused and looked from one to the other. He rubbed his chin. "I haven't heard either of you mention love."

Darrell had an answer ready. "Pastor … it was love that gave me hope. It was love that wouldn't allow me to move on with my life or to get involved with another woman. I love Jade. Everything that makes her who she is. The good, the bad and everything in between."

Jade had heard Darrell say he loved her many times. But this time it was different. Hearing it phrased that way brought tears to her eyes. "I … I never … really knew … what love was until recently." She turned to Darrell. "I know that it's a gift from God in the form of you." She choked and couldn't continue speaking. Darrell took Jade's hand and squeezed it tightly.

Pastor Jones cleared his throat. "I believe you love each other and I believe your love *is* a gift from God.

And therefore, what God hath joined together, let no man put asunder."

Darrell leaned forward. "Can we do it today?"

"I don't see why we can't. You gave me the license yesterday and everything is in order. And, from what you shared with me on yesterday, it's probably best."

Jade shot Darrell a look. "Today? When?"

Pastor Jones didn't miss a beat. "What about right after service?"

Darrell smiled, as if he'd had nothing to do with the idea. "That sounds great to me. We can have a large wedding later for our family and friends."

"I don't mind performing it twice."

Jade's mind was spinning. She'd come to church today so that the announcement could be made of her upcoming nuptials, not to actually have the ceremony performed.

"I'd like to call my mother. Maybe she can ..."

"Your mother will be here. So will all our close friends. I asked them to come today."

Jade tilted her head to one side. "You set me up?"

"Baby ... I ..."

She smiled. "It's okay, Darrell. I knew something was up yesterday at the beauty salon."

Darrell returned her smile. "I know you're no fool."

She took a deep shaky breath. "I meant what I said. I'm ready to marry you."

"Good. Both of you agree. I'll perform the ceremony right after morning service. I want you both to sit in the front row today.

ÓŒþ

Darrell and Jade sat in the front row as Pastor Jones instructed, and both of them tried to enjoy the sermon;

but today it was hard to focus on what was being said. Jade was nervous. She'd known it would be a very short engagement; nevertheless, she hadn't woken up that morning with becoming Darrell's wife on her agenda.

It was near the end of the sermon and Pastor Jones hadn't preached more than twenty minutes when he said, "We have a special mission today. It's hard to ignore the two people sitting together here in Cathedral."

The pastor looked at Jade and Darrell and Jade in turn looked over her shoulder in search of familiar faces. She saw her mother and sister first. Her mother smiled and winked as Theashia waved. Moments later, she found her son sitting between Darrell's parents.

Jade's attention was drawn to the choir loft when she heard the gasp of anticipation coming from somewhere in that direction. The whispering began to carry throughout the church.

Darrell took her hand and leaned close to her ear, "Are you ready?"

She nodded her reply as she directed her attention back to the pastor.

"I believe, wholeheartedly, that God has truly brought them together. They've asked me to join them in holy matrimony. They've expressed to me that they've waited long enough and are ready to begin a new life together. And so in just a few minutes … I'm going to give the benediction to signal the end of this morning's worship service. Then we'll prepare to join together in marriage, minister in waiting Darrell Parker Jr., and Jade Marie Sanders." The congregation began to clap. "Stand up, you two, and face the church."

By the time Jade and Darrell faced the congregation they was giving them a full ovation. Pastor Parker moved from the pulpit to the floor, positioning himself between them. The people continued to clap. Shouts of "Amen!" and "About time!" could be heard coming from the crowd. It seemed the clapping lasted forever.

Once the congregation settled down enough for the pastor to speak, he informed everyone that they were welcome to stay and witness the marriage.

After the benediction was administered, Jade was taken back to the pastor's study where Jade's mother, Theashia, Ivy, Sheena and Miranda had gathered. Darrell was taken to another room.

As soon as Jade laid eyes on Ivy, she wagged her finger at her. "When this is over, I'm going to get you."

Ivy burst out in laughter. "Why me? I wasn't the only one to be part of this conspiracy."

"No, but you were the ringleader. This thing has your imprint all over it," Jade said, laughing.

"No, actually, that honor goes to your future husband. We all just agreed to help him pull this off."

Jade looked over at her mother. "I guess you were a part of this, too?"

"I didn't know a thing. I was told on Friday to be here because your engagement was being announced, and that's all! Then Ivy called me this morning and told me it was possible that you would get married today."

Jade looked at Theashia and she threw her hands in the air. "I promise you, sis, I didn't know a thing. You know I would have told you."

Jade shook her head, wonderingly.

"Well, do you want to get married or what?" her mother asked.

"Yes, I want to get married, and I'm just glad all of you are here."

Miranda teased. "Oh, no! I do believe I see a tear forming in her eye."

Jade was known for her hard exterior, so none of them hardly ever saw the soft side of her. It was a revelation to everybody. "I'm just happy, that's all."

Ivy stood and motioned for Miranda to help give Jade the garment bag hanging on a hook on the wall. "I have a dress for you."

Jade's eyes widened when she saw it was the same dress she and Ivy had looked at the day before when they left the beauty salon. "How in the world did you …"

Ivy interrupted her. "Don't ask any questions. Just be happy you have the dress you liked so much!"

Jade hugged Ivy and kissed her cheek. She'd planned to buy the dress herself, but Ivy had talked her out of it, saying she should look at others first. They'd shopped and shopped, but Jade still liked the first one best, and had been nearly unbearably disappointed when they returned to find it already sold. Now it was clear why: Ivy had purchased the dress for Jade when she was in the dressing room.

Miranda opened a bag and pulled out a box. "I got the shoes, and they better fit," she said. She led Jade to the couch on the opposite side of the room. "Sit right here and try them on." After the shoes were on her feet, Miranda instructed her to stand up. "How do they feel?"

"Like a perfect fit."

"Yes!" Miranda yelled in triumph.

Jade's mother took the pearls from her neck and placed them around Jade's. "Now I understand why the Lord told me to wear these. Now you have something borrowed, 'cause I sure want them back."

Jade smiled. "Thanks, Mom."

"I hope you got the garter, Sheena." Ivy said.

Sheena reached into her purse and removed a small white bag. "Yes, I do, and it's blue."

Jade was getting misty all over again. "You guys thought of everything."

"Well, almost," Ivy said. "You don't have a ring for Darrell yet, do you?"

"You didn't!" Jade gasped.

Ivy laughed, "No, I didn't. However, when I mentioned it to your mother early this morning, she said she thought she could handle that."

Jade turned to look at her mother, tears in her eyes. "This was your father's ring. I'm sure he'd want you to have it. This is not borrowed. It's yours to give to Darrell."

Jade truly did cry now. The expression of love from her mother moved her to tears of joy. She didn't have any words for her, just a huge tight hug.

It took thirty minutes to get Jade dressed and ready to become Mrs. Darrell Parker Jr.

಑ಖಌ

Pastor Jones sent a member from his church to Pastor Owens' to let him know that Jade and Darrell were tying the knot. Owens was given the message by note and, just before he gave the benediction, he informed his congregation. He had no doubt that many of Jade's students would want to go, so he made the church vans available to the youth department.

Once Owens' members began to arrive, the church was bursting from the seams. Folding chairs were lined around the room and placed anywhere one could be placed. But by the time the wedding started, it was standing-room-only.

Once the wedding had been performed, Darrell and Jade stood in the atrium greeting their witnesses when Desmond ran to his parents, leaped into his father's arms, and said loudly, "Grandma says you can live at my house with me and Mommy now, Daddy!"

Everyone laughed, and Darrell hugged Desmond tightly to him. "Yes, son. I can stay in *your* house now."

Under the direction of Mother Brown, Jade's students decorated the church social hall while photos were being taken in the sanctuary.

Jade and Darrell couldn't believe the feast that was prepared for them by the women of the church. A professional caterer couldn't have done it better. The Cathedral women had been told by the pastor that he wanted to have an engagement dinner for the couple after morning service – exactly what they would have had, if Jade hadn't agreed to get married immediately.

Ivy had called the bakery the morning before and had ordered a five-tier wedding cake. She felt in her heart of hearts that this dinner would turn out to be Darrell and Jade's wedding reception. However, if her premonition had been incorrect, they could still have had it – as five separate cakes for dessert.

The bride and groom cut the cake and Jade couldn't resist smearing a little on Darrell's face. She threw the bouquet – and Ivy caught it. Darrell tossed the garter and Jason grabbed it; soon after, he walked out of the church.

Darrell had been ready to leave as soon as he heard the words pronouncing Jade as his wife coming from the pastor's lips. That had been over three hours ago. He whispered to his wife, "I'm ready to go."

Jade nodded, "I am, too. Let me find the girls so I can let them know we're leaving."

"They'll know we're gone when they don't see us."

Jade smiled at Darrell. "I won't be long."

"I'm timing you!" he yelled after her, pointing at his watch.

It wasn't long before Jade found them in the choir room. Miranda was sitting in a chair, Ivy was standing in the middle of the floor watching Sheena pace. "What's going on?"

"Jason," Miranda blurted out.

Jade didn't understand. "What are you talking about?"

"He caught the garter then left," Miranda clarified.

"Well, he probably has a plane to catch. He only came down for the weekend, right?"

"Yeah, and his plane doesn't leave until tomorrow morning," Sheena replied, miserably.

"Sheen …"

"Jade, don't worry. You go be with your new husband. We'll handle this."

She looked from one face to the other. "I only wanted you guys to know we were leaving."

Miranda got up and hugged Jade. "Be happy and blessed."

Ivy was next, "Congratulations, and God bless your union."

Sheena stood and gazed at her for a moment and hugged her tightly, not saying one word.

Jade pulled back first, "I'll be praying for you."

Sheena nodded her reply.

Ivy opened the door widely. "Now, get out of here and go knock some boots."

The room burst into laughter.

CHAPTER SIXTEEN

It was Tuesday. Five o'clock in the evening. In just one hour Jade would be forced to face her past.

On the morning after her wedding, Jade became nervous. Why had God allowed this man to cause such a disturbance in her life? She and Darrell sat in Conference Room A of William K. Hart the third's law office. After reading a portion of the report Vincent Marshall had put together, memories from sixteen years ago flashed in her mind.

Bill had asked Marshall – who was his law partner and best friend – to help him get as much information as possible about Keith Strickland. Bill was involved because Ivy had asked him to help. Of course, knowing how close Ivy and Jade were, he wanted to help. Getting Vincent Marshall involved was the right thing to do; his expertise was in family law.

Looking at the information in the report made Jade reminisce on the most agonizing time in her life. Running her fingers through the curls in her hair she looked over at Marshall. "This is costing a lot; isn't it?"

Marshall smiled. "Well you know I don't like to work for free. But after Bill and Ivy told me what was going on, I had to give some in-kind service."

"Jade." She turned to Bill as he spoke. "Don't worry. You'll never see a bill."

The phone rang and Bill picked it up. "Send them right in." He looked at Jade. "Your mother and Sheena are on their way up."

Jade was startled; no one had told her that her mother was coming; but she was more than relieved to see her. "Hi, Mama."

Her mother kissed her cheek. "You didn't tell me about this."

"I didn't want to worry you. I was going to handle it without you. I don't want you under any more stress than you have to."

"You've always been thoughtful, Jade. Always. You need to stop putting so much pressure on yourself. But, I don't think I'll have to worry about that anymore." She looked over at Darrell. "He's going to take good care of you."

"Yes, Mama, I'm sure you're right."

She turned to Sheena. "I see you are a woman of your word. You promised you'd be here… thank you."

"You know I couldn't leave you hanging. I know how important this is."

"Is Mama here because of you?"

Sheena shrugged. "I picked her up, but it was Darrell who invited her."

Jade gave her friend a weak smile. "I've never been this nervous in my whole life."

"Not even when you said *I do*?"

"Not even then."

Keith and his mother arrived at five minutes to six. Introductions were made and everyone shook hands;

Jade, alone, stayed in her seat, her lips pressed tightly together.

Keith noticed immediately. "Jade."

She paused before saying, "Keith." There was contempt in her voice.

Darrell began by saying. "I promised you we would meet and…"

Keith interrupted him. "Yeah, but I didn't know you were going to have a dream team with you."

"These are Jade's friends."

"I understand that, but this was supposed to be a friendly meeting between us," Keith said, reasonably.

"This is a friendly meeting. None of these attorneys are being paid. They are here supporting a friend."

This is ridiculous, Jade thought. "Let's cut to the chase," she said. "What do you want, Keith?"

He looked at her. "I want the opportunity to develop a relationship with my daughter."

"Why?" Darrell asked.

"What do you mean, why? She's my daughter," Keith retorted.

Jade shook her head. "Oh, so now you have a child, after all these years?"

"This was your doing, not mine. You decided to bring that child into the world."

"That's right, I did! And with the help of my parents, she's had a wonderful life." Remembering the whole awful experience, Jade stood up. "We never asked you for anything, not a crumb or cracker and you have the nerve …"

Jade's mother saw where this was going and interrupted her before it got too foul. "Jade!"

Jade couldn't believe the Stricklands had the audacity to come to this meeting. Marshall pushed a folder in front of Keith and his mother. "I think you need to take a look at these documents. It's my understanding that you all initiated the adoption by hiring your own lawyer to sever all paternal rights."

Keith opened the folder and looked at the document on top.

"Your parents filed this two weeks before your eighteenth birthday. However, it wasn't signed until a day after your birthday. Not only did your parents sign, but you did too. You'll find a transcript in that file of a meeting you had on that day without the presence of your parents telling you that you didn't have to sign this document. It further explained that your parents' signatures didn't mean anything and you had the opportunity to change your mind. But you elected to sign anyway. You also knew you had time to change your mind and during that time you never did."

Keith didn't say a word in his own defense. After looking through the folder he closed it and pushed it away from him. "All documents have a loophole."

"This one had plenty. But they're all closed now. Mr. and Mrs. Sanders used your attorney to prepare the adoption papers. He made sure that after you didn't exercise your right to change your mind during the allotted time, you never could."

"I never agreed to give up the baby. Never," Jade said sternly. "My mother and father told me that I was still their daughter and they would help me raise the baby. They didn't ask me to sign her over to them so they could adopt her. It was my idea. They didn't want to do it. They told me they were ready to be grandparents."

Jade looked around at all the people listening to her. "I had been praying for a solid week. I wanted an answer from God and I told Him I wouldn't stop praying until He answered me and He did. He placed His goodness into my parents' hearts and made them her parents, too, and me her big sister. That's what I've been ever since, a big sister."

"I understand that you reap what you sow," Mrs. Strickland said calmly. "My husband and I made a huge mistake when we took fate into our own hands." She looked directly at Jade. "We were ignorant. We thought we were protecting our son. But what we did was alienate ourselves from something more precious. A part of our lineage."

Keith tried to caution his mother to stop talking, but she ignored him.

"What's done is done. There's nothing we can do about the past. We can only look to the future." She stood up. "We were told by three different lawyers that we didn't stand a chance. I don't want to fight. I was woman enough to make my mistakes, and I must be woman enough to take the consequences. Jade, I must say, you are truly amazing. I knew you as a caterpillar, and now I see you as a beautiful black butterfly." She turned to Jade's mother. "You're a good-hearted woman, Nora. Always have been. I'm glad you were chosen to raise my granddaughter. Maybe in time you'll allow us to get to know her."

She pushed the chair she was sitting in up to the table. "Thank you for meeting with us, but I think it's best that we go." She looked at her son who hadn't moved. "Keith, let's go." He looked over at Jade and Jade stared right back at him.

"Just remember, there's always a loophole," he snarled.

"Be careful that you don't hang yourself searching for it," Jade retorted.

Keith walked out before his mother. "Don't worry about him. He'll need a little time to get over this."

"Thank you, Mrs. Strickland."

She smiled and walked out of the conference room.

Jade blew out a sigh of relief, turned and looked at her friends. "Do you think it's over?"

It was her mother who answered. "It will never be over until Theashia knows the whole truth."

"But …"

"Not now. We'll have to figure out when. But not now."

CHAPTER SEVENTEEN

Jade saw Miranda and Ivy sitting in the non-smoking section of Taco Palace. She figured they didn't think she would show up at their weekly gathering, opting to hang out instead with her new husband.

"Surprise!"

"Oh, snap, you won," Miranda said looking at Ivy.

"That's right, pay up."

"Won what?" Jade asked as she pulled out a chair next to Miranda's.

"Ivy said you would be here and I said you wouldn't."

"Oh … I see."

"I mean you haven't been married a week yet. I just figured you'd want to be with Darrell."

"I see Darrell every day. I don't get to see you all everyday."

Miranda smiled. "I feel so honored. You didn't put us down for a man."

"No, never!"

Ivy leaned over. "I meant to comment on your boyfriend, Randi. He's handsome."

"Yeah, well, he's not my boyfriend. We're just friends."

"Well, all relationships start out as friends."

"No, we'll never be anything but friends. He's not into heavyweight sisters." She sounded sad.

"How do you know? Did he tell you that?"

"No, he didn't come right out and say it. But I can just tell."

Jade shook her head. "Well, you could be wrong."

"Believe me, I'm not. And the craziest thing is, I don't want to know. I've met his grandmother and we've become fast friends. Could be that was his purpose in my life. To introduce me to such a wonderful woman of God."

"Is his grandmother in the ministry?"

"No, but she has the gift of prophesy. She told me that I could run, but I couldn't hide. God would get what he wanted out of me."

"Do you know what's she's talking about?" Jade asked

"Yeah." She paused. "It's something I never told anyone."

"And that is?" Ivy was watching her, fascinated.

"My call into the ministry."

Jade leaned back in her chair. "Oh, I knew that."

"I did, too. I've been wondering when *you* were going to accept it."

"You *knew* I'd been called?"

"Randi, it's not very hard to see that no matter how you try, you're just different from us ordinary people."

Miranda was silent. "You all never said anything."

"Well, now that you have confirmation from a complete stranger, maybe now you can talk to Dad."

"Hmm. I'm not exactly ready for that."

"Suit yourself. I sleep well at night. You're the one tossing and turning." Ivy turned to Jade. "So, how is married life?"

"To be honest, nothing has changed except we sleep together."

"That only means you had very little adjusting to do."

"Well, I think we're going to have a lot of adjusting to do and real soon too."

"Why is that?"

"Well, your father called us to the church last evening. We met with him, Pastor Grady, Pastor Williams and Pastor Thomas. They informed us that Pastor Owens had resigned and Pastor Thomas was taking over his congregation."

She gasped. "Pastor Thomas has to be … what? Ninety?"

"No, he's eighty-two. But the catch is they want Darrell to work with him as assistant pastor to learn under a seasoned pastor."

"They're preparing him to pastor? That's spectacular!" Ivy exclaimed.

Jade nodded. "Your father's idea."

"What about the school Owens was trying to start?"

"Oh, that's the other thing. They still want me to take over as headmistress."

"So are you?"

"Darrell thinks I should."

Ivy nodded vigorously. "You're good at teaching. You're good with kids, period."

"What I want to know is, why did Owens resign?"

"From what we were told, he and his wife has decided to divorce and he wants to leave the area soon as possible."

"His wife finally got enough of his mess," Miranda huffed. "I never liked that man. He's a hypocrite and I told you all so."

Jade looked at Miranda. "You know, I'm so glad that God is not like man."

"Well, you know I'm telling the truth. The man is a two-timing dog."

"Yes, and it's a good thing God is a God of a second chance."

"Third and fourth if you need it," Ivy commented.

"Why are you taking up for him?" Miranda asked.

Jade thought about Owens and his confession to her. His admissions made her take a good look at her own dilemma, influencing her own decision. "'Cause I feel compassion for him. I think he's taking this opportunity to correct some things in his life, and maybe just maybe, he and his wife will be able to find true happiness through it all."

"So are you saying you don't believe in until death do you part?"

"What God joins together, yes. But not when man puts himself with someone. That's the reason why we have so many divorces in the church, because we rush to the altar on our own without consulting God. So I believe what God joins together is until death do you part."

"You know..." Ivy shook her head, "...you have a point there."

Miranda blew out a sigh. "Well, I never looked at it that way."

Jade hunched her shoulders. "God never fails, that's all I know."

"Well, I guess Darrell will have to reschedule his trial sermon."

"Yeah, that was done as well." Jade smiled. "He'll be delivering it on Sunday."

"This Sunday coming?" Ivy asked with surprise.

Jade nodded. "This was the original date before he asked to have it cancelled, so it's working out for him in spite of all the drama."

"I hate to say it, but you do know that Pastor Thomas is not a well man," Miranda remarked.

"We were told. Your father said that since Darrell will be completing his theology degree in May, and Pastor Thomas has him under his wing, that Darrell will be more than ready to step in his place within a year or so."

"Well, my father's been doing this a long time and he's a good judge of people. And beside, I know Darrell is real about his calling."

"I agree," Miranda concurred.

"On another note, Bill gave me the blow-by-blow commentary on last Tuesday's showdown."

"I'm sure he did. And Vincent Marshall is a jewel!"

"Yeah well, I was surprised that he participated. He never does anything for free. Just be glad you're Sheena's friend."

"Why you say that?"

"'Cause he's wants Sheena, and I do believe it's the only reason why he agreed – knowing she would be there. At least that's what Bill told me."

Jade looked around her. "Where's Sheena, anyway?"

Miranda tossed her head. "She said she was working late."

"She and Jason settle things between them?"

"He's still a Muslim – so, no," Miranda answered.

Jade looked from one woman to the other. "What about Josephine?"

"What about her?" Ivy asked.

"I know they work together, but she's not hanging with her, is she?"

"No, I'm sure that's a done deal." Ivy said.

"I think it's a done deal with Jason too." Miranda added.

Jade looked confused. "Why do you say that?"

Miranda shrugged. "She doesn't have a choice. The man serves a different God."

"You're probably right. It would never work." Jade shook her head sadly. "However, there are some things that only God can straighten out."

Ivy's cell phone rang. "Well, only time will tell. Hello?" Ivy paused to listen and when Miranda began to say something to Jade Ivy held up her hand to stop her. "What?" Her eyes grew large. "When? I mean, I just talked to her a few hours ago." The alarm in Ivy's voice was unmistakable. She reached for her pocketbook. "No, I'm with Jade and Randi."

"What's going on?" Jade asked in a panic.

Ivy threw fifty dollars on the table, "Gather your things." She instructed to her friends in a whisper as she put on her coat.

"What's going on?" Miranda almost shouted as they headed for the door.

Ivy pointed in the direction of her car gesturing to her friends to follow her. "We're on our way right now."

"What's going on?" Miranda and Jade asked as they walked briskly through the parking lot.

"Sheena was in some sort of accident."

"What? Where is she?" Jade asked alarmed.

"I'm already praying," she said to the caller. "We're getting across Ben Franklin Bridge as fast as humanly possible." Ivy closed her cell phone.

"Was she in her car?" Miranda wanted to know as they reached Ivy's car.

Ivy ignored Miranda. "Leave your car here, Jade, we'll pick it up later."

"Would you please tell us what's going on?" Jade asked as she got into the car.

"If I knew I'd tell you. All I know is her mother said she was brought there unconscious. They think she was hit in the parking garage."

ᏋᎧᏣᎹ

Jade, Miranda and Ivy reached Temple University Hospital with record speed. As soon as they arrived in the emergency room, Sheena's mother and father stood up to greet them. Sheena's mother was shaking and in tears.

"What's happened?" All the girls asked almost in unison.

Mr. Daniels spoke because his wife couldn't. "The police said it wasn't an accident. They said she was beaten."

"Oh, my God. Who would want to hurt her?" Miranda asked.

"That's what the police asked us. I don't know anyone who hates her so much they would want to beat her the way they say she's been beaten."

"I assume it's pretty bad?" Jade asked.

"They just took her up to surgery. The doctor said they have to relieve the pressure on her brain."

All the girls gasped. Jade broke down in tears.

It took Ivy only a moment to know what they had to do. "No!" she shouted. Everyone looked at her. "We don't have time to cry and feel sorry. It's time to pray," Ivy said, wiping her eyes.

"You're right. She's in surgery and we have to be vigilant. We're in spiritual warfare."

Ivy grasped Mr. Daniels' hand. He took his wife's hand. Jade grasped Mrs. Daniels' hand and Miranda's with the other, forming a circle. Pastor Jones and his wife walked in the room just in time to join the circle for prayer.

Miranda started praying without being asked. "Father, if there is anything in me that would hinder this prayer, please forgive me now for anything that I've done that's unpleasing in your sight."

"Forgive us, Lord," several people said.

"I need you to hear me, Lord. Hear my cry, please hear my plea."

"In the name of Jesus." The words were whispered in the air.

"We don't know the situation. We don't know the facts. All we know is you are merciful and your love reaches from everlasting to everlasting. We know that you can meet the doctor in the operating room and you can guide his hand. Nobody knows the physical anatomy like you, Lord."

"Yes, Lord," Sheena's mother wept.

"For you are the creator, the author and finisher of everything. You said one can chase a thousand and two can put ten thousand to flight. Well, Lord there is seven of us here and we are asking you to bind the enemy, in the name of Jesus. Let the doctor come back with a good report. Allow a miraculous healing just like you did for the woman with an issue of blood. Just like you did for the centurion soldier's servant, please … heal … and deliver."

When Miranda paused, Jade took over. "We are asking you to honor our prayer our Lord. Grant Sheena your favor. Just because she loves you, grant her your favor; just because she's your child, grant her your favor because you are obligated by your word to take care of her. We are asking you to protect her as of this moment. I've not seen the righteous forsaken nor his seed begging bread. We know … that if you be for her … it's more than the whole world against her ... You are … our strength … and our redeemer." Jade was sobbing and unable to continue.

Ivy began. "Father, let nothing hinder our prayer. Examine our hearts. For we know you see past the words from our lips and see the intentions of our hearts. Search us like only you can … and let our hearts speak ... like only they can." Ivy looked up to the ceiling. "Don't take her…away…"

"Please, Father …" the group begged.

"Restore her, make her whole in every way. Don't take her, please … please."

Mrs. Daniels cried out in pain. "Jesus! Oh, Jesus … Lord … Jesus …"

Ivy's dropped her head. "Amen."

Dear Reader:

I hope you've enjoyed **JADE'S DILEMMA: Lead Us Not Into Temptation** and looking forward to **SHEENA'S DILEMMA: It's Better To Marry Than To Burn**.

Some may think I was a little preachy in this story, other may think this story was simply more scripture driven. But whatever your thoughts, I pray you were entertained and that you have learned a thing or two through the Word of God in the process.

Pastor Preston Owens is just begging to have his own story told. I'm interested in knowing what you think. Drop me a line and tell me if you think Pastor Owens should have his own story added to the Dilemmas Series.

In the meantime, I'm working on Sheena's Dilemma due to be released September 2007.

Until next time, may God continue to bless and keep you.

Peace,

Reign
P.O. Box 4731
Rocky Mount, NC 27803-0731

On the Web:
www.Reign.NickiAngela.net
Reign@NickiAngela.net

ABOUT THE AUTHOR

Reign is the pseudonym used by an author who lives in North Carolina that works at a Housing Authority in a position that allows her to make a positive impact on the lives of others.

Reign lives with her husband and four of her six children.

An Anthology From Dreams Books

All In The Family
By: Janice Sims, Maxine Thompson & Melanie Schuster
ISBN 0-9770936-3-8

The Johnson sisters haven't been home to tiny Mason Corners, South Carolina for a long time. Their mother, Sara, feeling neglected, gives them an ultimatum: Come to the family reunion...OR ELSE!!!

In Janice Sims's MOMMA'S BABY, DADDY'S MAYBE, perfect wife and mother, Candace, 41, of Charleston, has to come to terms with the nasty paternity rumors that have been making the rounds in the family since she was a child. And Angela, 25, a super-model wannabe in Miami wants to come home, but what will the man she left behind do when she tells him what she had to do to survive while they were apart?

In WHERE MY HEART IS **Melanie Schuster** gives us a glimpse into the life of A-personality Sharon, 32, a successful New York City television producer who has excelled at everything she's ever tried. What drives her to always be on top? And in striving for perfection has she missed the signals her handsome co-worker has been sending for two years now? She finds out when she asks him to pose as her man at the family reunion.

And in **Maxine Thompson's** SUMMER OF SALVATION Debra, 35, a casting director in Hollywood brings her Mexican-American husband home for the first time. They eloped, and her mother has never forgiven her for it. Will her mother be able to get over hurt feelings? Or will there be a showdown during the festivities?

Whatever happens at the Johnson Family Reunion, you know that it will be kept... ALL IN THE FAMILY

More From Dreams Books

Ivy's Dilemma – Thy Will Be Done (Dilemma Series Book #1)
a novel by Reign
ISBN 0-9770936-0-3

Retired professional football player Raymond Miller tells his childhood sweetheart Ivy Jones-Miller to divorce him after 11 years of marriage. Before the papers can be filed Raymond is killed in an automobile accident. Ivy's faith is tested as secrets are revealed and she is forced to deal with opposition from her In-laws. Through her faith and the love of her family and friends Ivy is able to survive the heartbreak and the scrutiny forced on her after her husband's untimely death.

From Crack Addict To Pastor
a true story by Karen Sills
ISBN 0-9770936-3-8

Pastor Karen Sills describes her years of substance abuse in this dramatized rendition of her life. She gives detailed accounts of how drug addiction impacted her and the lives of the people she loves dearly. Through this book she shows just how merciful God is. And because of His mercy and grace, she is delivered from prostitution, lesbianism, imprisonment and drug addiction.

Perfect Love
a novel by Arsoleen Woolcock
ISBN 0-9770936-4-6

Breanna's one dream is to find that special love by a man who's as wonderful as her father. But the secret that has been hidden for years surfaces likely to destroy her dreams of forever after in a Perfect Love.

The Homecoming (Mt. Hope Series Book #1)
a novel by Angela Santana
ISBN 0-9770936-7-0

Tragedy turns to blessing when a despondent, desperate young pioneer woman finds herself alone and in crisis in an unfamiliar place. Faced with a decision she never thought she'd have to make, she learns that God's grace is not just sufficient but abounding, and that all things work together for good if only she can learn to trust...

www.ingramcontent.com/pod-product-compliance
Lightning Source LLC
Chambersburg PA
CBHW050930120626
46552CB00001B/125